JASON JOHNSON was born in Enniskillen in 1969 and has lived in Belfast, England and the USA. He has been a barman, a shoe-salesman, a car washer, a supermarket employee, a waiter, a courier, a chair-ride operator, an apprentice stonemason, and a painter and decorator. As a freelance journalist, he worked for the *Irish News* and *Belfast Telegraph* before taking the News Editor position at the *Irish Sunday People*, which he left in 2004. He lives in Belfast. He currently describes himself as a writer.

G000161589

WOUND LICKER

JASON JOHNSON

THE
BLACKSTAFF
PRESS
BELFAST

Sincere thanks to Damian Keenan for making everything work. This story wouldn't be here without him. Thanks also to Greg Harkin for his contacts, and to Joe Polizzi, Alex McGreevy and Shane Donaghey for the advice. Thanks to my family for saying 'go for it' and to Sinead for being all that she is. Huge thanks as well to Blackstaff Press for being so darned creative and cool, and especially to Rachel McNicholl. Her sure-fire counsel, vigilance and courage progressed everything, and helped a writer live a dream. And thanks to Belfast, where life is good.

The events, passions and city which inspired this story are real. The characters are the product of the author's imagination, and any resemblance to actual persons is purely coincidental. Some locations are real, some are not.

First published in 2005 by
Blackstaff Press
4c Heron Wharf, Sydenham Business Park
Belfast BT3 9LE
with the assistance of
The Arts Council of Northern Ireland

ARTS
COUNCIL
of Northern Ireland

Typesetting by Red Barn Publishing, Skeagh, Skibbereen
Printed in England by Cox and Wyman

A CIP catalogue record for this book is available
from the British Library

ISBN 0–85640–774–7

www.blackstaffpress.com

For those who work
to make it better

HMG SECURE INTERNAL MAILING SYSTEM

SENDER: GSB
RECIPIENT: UNDISCLOSED
SUBJECT: WOUNDLICKER
LEVEL: TOP SECRET — EYES ONLY

April 12, 2004

Sir,

Please find attached the complete Woundlicker report from Station D6 as requested.

Regards,
GSB

INTERNAL RESEARCH REPORT

SOURCE STATION: D6
OPERATION: WOUNDLICKER
CLASSIFICATION LEVEL: TOP SECRET

COMMENTS:
This material has been transcribed from intelligence
gathered at Listening Post D6–14, Belfast, Northern
Ireland. Communications intercepted between March 09
and March 20, 2004.

Well, how's life? Taking it easy, are you? I bet you are. Sure you couldn't get it any easier than sitting on your arse all day. Wish I could do the same, so I do. You must have the best job ever. Ack well. So what's the crack, anyway? What dirty pies are your dirty wee fingers in today?

I have to wonder about people like you. I was thinking, you must just sit there all day waiting to hear a wee nugget of information. I bet you think you're a hero and all, don't you? I bet you do. You're not. I mean that. I mean, what's a hero doing sitting on his hole all day?

God, you must hear a pile of shite. Shagging and shouting and crying and lying and laughing and all that useless bollocks. That's all that really goes on in private, so it is. Personal stuff. But it must be mad sometimes, eh? Just deciding if people are good guys or bad guys? Mental, so it is. I suppose you're right in one way. You can tell fucken everything about people by what they talk about, so you can. I tell you, you'd be interested in what I could talk about. A few wee nuggets there, all right. I'm not fucken joking.

Anyway, what about that Arab bastard? That's what I want to know, big lad. I don't suppose you could tell me anything about that? Maybe you don't even know anything. I don't know if you're even interested in Arabs and all them ones. But that's all I'd like to know, to be honest.

So give us a sign or something. Go on. Send someone round telling me the weather's nice in Russia on a Tuesday or some shite like that. Some wanker with a newspaper under his arm or a wee rose in his buttonhole. I'd love that. I'd laugh me head off, so I would.

Ack, fuck this. Laugh a minute, so you are. Laugh a minute. I'm away. I'd wish you all the best and all that, but I couldn't give a shite about you. Fuck you, mate.

How you doing? It's me again, Fletch the Wretch. I know,
I know, I didn't expect me back either. So how you been,
mucker? I'm grand, seeing as you ask so politely. Doing
just rightly under the circumstances. Still here, anyway.
Still alive. Life goes on and all that shite.

They're saying the Arabs are going to go crackers again.
They caught some fundamentals in London yesterday, so
they did. They reckon they were looking to nick a plane
and fly into something. Same group who did that bollocks
in Spain. September Eleven crowd. Mad bastards.

I had to laugh, so I did. They reckon they'd ram one
anywhere they could, just to kill Westerners and all that.
All the usual wankers from Belfast were on the radio this
morning. They were saying how we might be next. One
man was saying the Arabs could get an EasyJet in
England and ram it into the Hilton Hotel over here, or
into Stormont or somewhere. Load of bollocks, like.
What use is a bunch of dead wankers from Northern
Ireland to anyone? Who'd give a shite? Not fucken me
anyway.

People here just love getting excited about terrorism, so
they do. They can't resist it. I wish someone would crash a
plane here, to be honest. It'd make my day. Fuck, you'd
hear me laughing across the town. I'd be pissing myself,
like. I'd be standing there with them wee paddles directing
them in, for fuck's sake. Big plane sticking out of

Stormont? Happy days. You couldn't beat it. Warm me hands on the fire, so I would.

I swear to God, the people here. You should have heard them. They were saying how tough we all are, and that we know all about terrorism, and that it could never crush the spirit of the people of Ulster and all that. I never heard so much fucken shite in me life. They don't know what they're talking about.

See, when those mad Arabs go hunting? They don't take fucken prisoners. A couple of hundred dead in Spain and they were laughing. And what was it? Three thousand and odd in New York? All innocent as fuck, so they were, but the Arabs were laughing away again. Then down in Bali – another couple of hundred of tourists. The Arabs play in the major fucken league, so they do. And here's us sitting in our wee terrace houses in Northern Ireland, drinking tea and feeding the budgie and saying how much we know about it all. Get away to fuck with that.

Sure Omagh was the biggest bomb here in thirty-five years, and that was only about thirty people killed, fuck's sake. That wouldn't even have them Arabs smiling, so it wouldn't. When they talk about operations, they're not talking about a wee bunch of Taigs from the back arse of Derry blowing up a fucken Tesco warehouse or something. What the fuck is that about? The Arabs would be laughing at that, so they would. They'd be saying the ones here never even had the guts to strap themselves to a bomb and go for a mad wee dander.

I swear, I wish there had been a proper war in this kip. A proper fucken war. All this hiding behind hedges with remote controls, and wee timers on bombs and all that shite, and then running off to your Ma's house to pretend it wasn't you – it was pathetic. A proper war would have just got the shite out of the system, so it would. We just had a dirty wee squabble that left too many victims stumbling round the place half fucken mad and giving off shite about all the bastards they hate. It's like a halfway house for the half fucken dead round here.

Half the people in this town are fucked up in the head, so they are. They just love whingeing about this and that and voting for any loony who says he'll show that the bastards on the other side haven't a clue what they're on about. The job was never finished. Thirty-five years? I tell you, the Arabs wouldn't have left a thing standing. They don't give a shite what people think, so they don't. That's fucken terror, so it is. When you just can't buy them off, that's terror. This place could've done with some of that. At least then when the war ended, you'd know whether it was over or not.

To be honest, I don't give a fuck. I rise above all that. Fuck the scars and all. Fuck them ones who go round pretending they give a shite about people just because they're the same religion and all. It's all bollocks. This place is full of fucken liars.

You know the most excited any cunt here has ever been? It was after a load of their own people were killed, so it was. It's true. They loved it. They could then just go round shouting about how the other side were all cunts and get all the sympathy they wanted and all. It made their shite wee cause make sense to other people then, so it did. They'd go to strangers' funerals and all, just because of who killed them. Fuck's sake. That's all half the people here ever wanted. To be able to show everyone that the people on the other side were cunts.

Fuck it. It's history. Life is now, you know. That makes sense after all the shite I've had this last wee while. I'm just going to use me own time for me own stuff. Use me time right. I was sort of thinking about it, see? I was looking at the clock in work, at the wee second hand going round and round, and wondering what the fuck I was at. I swear, I just felt like taking it off the wall and going tick-tock back into its face, you know. Just giving it the time of day for a change. That'd be just like me, so it would – tick-tocking away to myself.

I'd say that's how all this shit happened. It's like I've had a bad reaction to Northern Ireland, and it's made me want to shout at fucken clocks and stuff. That's what I put it down to anyway. But at least I know it. At least I know I'm half crackers, not like the rest of the dickheads in this country. But I'll probably still end up an oul man wandering about the place and shouting at clocks.

But here, enough of that oul shite. That's not what I want to say. There's other stuff I'm going to tell you, right? But I want to say this here first. I don't mind talking to you. I don't. But you'll just have to let me say it the way I want to. I'm going to tell it all to you, so I am. So write it down or something. Tape it, or whatever.

Oh wait. Got to go. If I don't help guide that wanker onto the ramp we'll have another fucken death round here. Right then.

D6–14. March 12. Friday.
14.39
Speaker(s): Woundlicker

What about you, big balls? Sorry about running off yesterday, but the standard of driving round here is appalling. I swear to God. A dog could drive a car onto that ramp. Fucken disgrace, so it is.

I have to say I'm a pretty good driver, so I am. Lost the licence for being blocked one night and all, but it doesn't mean I lost the skills. Know what I mean? By the way, the civil service doesn't know about that, so say nothing. I'd be out on me arse if they knew. I never declared it. It was only a bit of bad luck, so it was. Christ, was I full that night or what? Drove someone's car right into a big red postbox. Bust the total fuck out of me face. See postboxes? Worse than walls, so they are.

Anyway, you don't need to know that. I'm going to tell you what you need to know, right? The rest is a waste of time.

So listen. Take this down. I'm going to tell you what happened last week, last Monday night. I'll try to get it all in some sort of order so it makes some kind of sense. That's the best way to tell it, and I make the rules. Fuck you if you don't like it.

Right. It was half two in the morning. I was sleeping like a wee baby. Fucken knackered, so I was. Then I heard this mad knocking. It sort of sprung me eyes open. It was like knocking and kicking and shouting and fucken banging and the whole lot, so it was. First I thought it was my door and me heart nearly exploded, but it wasn't. I know it was exactly half two because of that clock with the big green numbers beside me scratcher. This girl was shouting outside. She's roaring, like. She goes 'Let me fucken in' and shite like that. You know the sort of thing that time of night.

So I looked out the window anyway. I could see her at the door of a house on the road below. I live on the fourth floor of a big fuck-off block, so I overlook it all. It's a great view sometimes, I have to say. So this wee girl was blonde and wearing all black, and that's really all I could see. She was kicking at the door, wee terraced house, all the lights on. But she was sort of running out of steam. She's going 'Open fucken up' and all this, over and over. The neighbours must have heard it. I sleep well and I heard it all clear as day. I don't think anyone was looking except me. People don't want to look at people who go shouting round my way, so they don't. They're dead timid sometimes. It's weird that. Anyway, it was like it was just me and her for a wee minute.

It was funny too. She was drunk as a skunk. You ever try to do something when you're dead drunk and you're dying for a piss? You're useless at it. She was holding her wee cold legs together in her wee black skirt, bouncing up and down, bladder busting on her. To be honest, I thought it was a right sketch. I laughed, so I did. Either the guy in the house was asleep or else he just wasn't going to let the slapper in. I thought she might be about to piss herself, or that she might drop her knickers and have a slash there on the spot. That would've been magic. I'm a dirty fucker like that, so I am. Anyway, she was fit to blow. You can only hold the oul bladder for so long before you faint or something. You'd end up pissing yourself whatever way it worked out.

But forget all that. There was no fanny on show that night. But what happened was she was knocking so hard that she cracked one of the wee window panes on the door. There's like nine wee squares of glass. You know them kind of doors? So she busted this wee bit of glass. You could hear the crack when she did it. She was a wee bit shocked and sort of looked at it for a minute, but then she just went the whole way and put her fucken fist straight through it. I laughed, so I did. Tough wee lassie or what? I loved that. If she hadn't been busting for a piss she probably wouldn't have done it, to be honest. I don't know. So she smashed it anyway and then stuck her hand in and just opened the door, like burglars do. She sort of staggered on in and just left it lying wide open. I reckoned she'd be going to the bog right away, so I did.

Then seconds later and, I swear, there's shouting like you never heard in your life. I just stood there, buck naked, listening to it all pumping out of the house. I love shite like that. I couldn't make out a word, like. But I could hear the tempers and all. You could just tell there'd be a punch or a kick or some shit. The blood was up. I was standing looking for ages, so I was. As nosey as you, so I am. After a while it went all quiet. The lights were still on, but nothing else was coming from the house. The drink does that to people, I reckon. Switches them on and off. One minute you're all fired up and then a minute later you're dead to the world.

I didn't know how cold I was until I got back into bed. Me nuts were just like wee pebbles, so they were. It was freezing as fuck. The heating in my flat's a joke. The big fuck-you clock was just counting away with its big green glow all over the place. Two forty-two. I wasn't going to sleep after that. So to be honest, I just thought about going on a bit of a mission. I mean, fuck the time of day and all. I was more into the search for a wee bit of crack, you know? Don't judge me, like. Well, judge away if you want. I don't give a fuck. I was only being honest. I try to be honest. I'm probably not, but I try to be. Most of the time I am.

So I put on me clothes anyway, right? They were just lying around me room. I never get to the laundry. So I put on this oul blue sweater and cream trousers that I haven't worn in ages. It was like a way of disguising myself. I know it was useless, but that's what I did. For all I know they might have seen me before in the boiler suit, so this made me look different. I look like a wanker in that boiler suit, so I do. Who wouldn't, like? Anyway, don't worry about all that. I dressed different and went down in the lift and out the door and over the road. Nothing was happening inside the house. Nothing I could hear anyway. There wasn't a sinner about. Graveyard, so it was. So I says I'll just walk on in here to fuck.

The place smelled of booze and fags and fish and chips and shite like that. Minging. But everything smells like that round here. I was silent as a feather but it didn't matter. Those two weren't for waking. They were out for the count in the living room, pissed out of their heads. She was on the floor, all curled up, piss all over her skirt, and he was on a chair, like he'd just fallen back, blocked out of his head. There was blood and piss on both of them, so there was. I'd say they'd a good wee slap at each other. Her hair was all thrown up all over the show, just lying there, dead to the world. He was scratched up beside his eye. I mean, he was a big fat cunt and she was a tiny wee thing. Bad shit, like. At least she gave him something back, I reckoned. Fair play to her.

I'd seen your man before, hanging round the streets. I'd never seen her. A wee stranger, so she was. Her face was sort of hidden with the way she was lying, and her body was shivering a wee bit. It was freezing in there too, so it was. She looked dead on, but it was hard to tell. Nice wee tight body anyway. If her skirt had been hitched up any higher, I'd probably have done something dodgy. But I was scared of waking her, so I didn't. I'm just being honest.

So anyway, I looked round for a wee bit. If I'd seen some money, I'd have nicked it. It'd probably have been nicked off someone else anyway, knowing what kind of bastard lives round that place. Dirty money belongs to anyone who gets their hands on it, I reckon. But honest, I'd have taken jewellery or any oul shite and flogged it on. But there was fuck all to be had. If I'd been after an ugly porcelain statue with some porcelain roses or half a can of Harp with fag ash on it, then I'd have been sorted. Know what I mean? But I wasn't.

There was fuck all in the kitchen either. No food or nothing. I'd have nicked a can of beans, you know, just to get something, after getting dressed and going out and all. But there was fuck all food. I tell you, it really did stink. It was like an oul dog's home or some shite, but there was no dog there. I didn't go upstairs. I thought about it, but I didn't do it. There didn't seem to be any point. And that fat cunt could have blocked me way out if he'd come round anyway. A man like that'd kill you.

So I was going back out when I seen this newspaper on the table in the living room, just beside where fat arse was sleeping. There was something under it. You could see by the way it was sitting, sort of propped up. I just knocked the paper away and there was this gun. A pistol. A Browning. Black, heavy, solid-looking thing. Bigger than you'd think. Bigger than I'd think. And there was a phone too, a fancy wee blue mobile. I thought, fuck it, I'll have these. So the mobile and the gun went into the pockets, and I got the fuck out of there. I didn't even think about fingerprints or nothing. I'm no master criminal. But I did what I wanted and that was grand. Went home and slept like a nun's cunt after that.

Oh wait – worker on the loose.

All right, dickhead? How's it going? Any news from the front, eh? I was thinking there that it makes me feel half normal talking to some nosey British bastard like you, so it does. Me sitting talking bollocks and you sitting listening to it. Mad as fuck, the pair of us.

What kind of Brit are you anyway? Scottish, English, Welsh? Or maybe you're some zero hero from here trying to show Her Majesty that we're not all fuckers. I'd wish you good luck with that one, mate. Maybe you're a woman. Pardon me for being sexist. In that case you're a female bastard, whatever that is. A bitch or something. A bastette. Doesn't matter. You're still a lowlife.

But here. I know you're checking your watch and thinking oul Fletcher's burning the midnight oil in the oul Stormont garage. Hope I'm not keeping you back. Truth is, I'm not hurrying home, that's all. I'm casing the joint now I have it to myself. Couple of things I wanted to check. But you'll not mind that. Not that I'd give a fuck if you did anyway. You know me.

So aye, I was saying I'd been to Wee Blondie's house that night. So the next day I had to go to work. I was a bit knackered like, and a bit down. I usually wake up depressed as fuck. The way the dirty light comes in just makes my shite wee bedroom look like it's been dropped in the River Lagan, so it does. I remember I just wanted to get stuck into the drink right away. You know those days when you just want to be fucked with the drink as soon as you wake up? I could have downed a bottle of any oul shite for breakfast then and there. Gloomy as fuck, like. It just hit me that day, so it did.

And it was no better later on either. The Arab fucker was really pissing me off. Ack, I knew then that he was all right really, but he was just on one of his rolls. He was getting pissed off with the world and that meant everyone had to listen to him spouting. It's Karim I'm talking about here. The world famous Karim from Algeria. That's in north Africa, so it is. Hot as fuck, I'd say. That's why people round there are a bit darker. Not black, like. But well tanned, you know.

Karim was always reading his wee black Koran and praying, so he was. He'd get down on this dirty wee mat on his knees and face the petrol pump. Facing Mecca, he told me. I told him one time I couldn't give a fuck what he was facing or what he did on his wee mat. He was at it five times a day. It's a lot of work, like.

So anyway, he'd got off with some loyalist slapper that weekend, he was telling me. He'd been going round the pubs – he doesn't drink, like – and in one bar he'd met this Milly from up the Cregagh Road somewhere. I've no fucken idea how he got off with her. No girl with the gift of sight would've touched that toothless wanker. The smell of him would've knocked a fucken crane down.

Anyway, he gave her one back at her house. He was going on about it all that morning. He was saying she was a worthless whore and all this. He was saying because she shagged him that she was no good. He wouldn't give her a break all fucken morning. I never say much in the mornings, but I lost it after a couple of hours that day. He said Belfast women had no shame and all this shite. That riled me. I don't know why, but it riled me up big time.

I squared up to the cunt and told him I'd never shag one of his dirty Arab mingers because they've all got beards. And I said if I did, she'd have to have a bag on her head and that her hole would be covered with flies laying eggs and all that oul stuff. Usual oul crap, like. But he went fucken mad about me saying that, so he did. He actually jumped up in the air a wee bit because he was so angry, like. It was dead funny. The boys were calling him a Paki dickhead and all this. Then I told him he'd insulted Belfast women and I was just doing it back. Fair fucken play to me, like. Not that I give a fuck about any loyalist bitch from up the Cregagh Road, but I just wanted to make the point. He got it and all, but he didn't like to say he did.

So we made up after that, anyway. Two tuna sarnies and we were all pals again. But I tell you, I said to myself I'm going to watch this cunt from now on. I never really had a problem with Muslims or mad fundamentalists or any of that oul shite. They can kill all the fuckers of the day wherever they want. It's nothing to me. But there's a way sometimes people say things and it just annoys you. You feel it in your gut. Fuck knows why. It's an instinct thing. Good insults hit you in your stomach. So that had annoyed me anyway. He's lucky I didn't smash his fucken head in, so he is. He got away lightly. Anyway. Some character, oul Karim.

It was busy all day, so it was. It always is on a Tuesday. Most of the cars that've been out for the weekend have all ended up back with us by then and we're the mugs who have to clean the fucken things. All sorts of cars in all sorts of states. There's some dirty bastards work at Stormont, I can tell you. And they're not all just the low-grade civil servants either. The senior ones are smelly fuckers too, including the ministers and all. They just treat the cars like complete shite because they don't pay for them or clean them or anything. I'm fed up cleaning up after the bastards. And when it's your job to do it, that's bad news. I remember thinking to myself I was going to go and get hammered that night to get me mind off all the crap I had to do because of them bastards. I'd been thinking about the drink all fucken day and I couldn't wait.

So I went on home anyway. The bus pulled up near the shops and I got off. It was fucken pissing rain all round me, down me neck and everywhere. I was soaking. I think it was the rain made me want to drink as much as work did. Muggins here has no umbrella or hat or any fucken thing like that. I never learn, like. And it had been raining for fucken ages too. Three full days, more or less.

I went into the off-licence anyway. There was about five sad, wet, angry-looking bastards in there all thinking the same thing as me. Whiskey will do the job, I reckoned, even though it tastes like shite. It's not so bad when it's a hot whiskey though, with those wee brown things floating in it. So anyway, I got some whiskey and picked up some Belgian beer, about 5 per cent, and bought that too. I'd had it before. Tastes a bit shitty, but then I'm no expert. But it's supposed to be good stuff, so fuck it, it'll do the job. Some wanker with his lip pierced served me. Eighteen quid. I felt like smashing the bottle over his fucken head.

Those shops are a joke, I swear to God. You're always hearing about some Prod dickhead getting his head kicked in there, or some Catholic getting a doing. You know the shops? The ones near the Peaceline in Ardoyne, north

Belfast. I can see the Peaceline from out the window of me flat. And I'm telling you, it just keeps getting bigger. It was smaller when the Troubles were on, and when the ceasefires came they made it bigger because there was more sectarian shite on the streets than ever. Less people were being shot and all, so people just started getting cheekier with each other and there was more fights. That wall can make you feel like you live in a box sometimes. I used to feel sorry for those ones who have that thing at the back of their houses, but I don't now. They're the ones who want it at the end of the day. They're the ones who won't sort their own shite out. So they fucken deserve it.

Anyway there's this wee set of shops, right? Newsagent, offie, laundrette and a couple of other places. Credit Union or some shit. I have as little to do with those places as possible. Banks and all that. All fucken bad news. So anyway, everyone has to use the shops now and then. There's fuck all else. Everyone needs bread and vodka and shite. The shops are sort of closer to the Taig end, so there's always more Fenians hanging round the place. But sometimes the Prods gather a few wankers together and go and stand there too.

There's always shite going on there anyway. Remember the other night, when that wanker lost an eye? He was belted by some Orange cunts, so he was. The fucker had it coming. I know the guy to see and I know rightly he's the first bastard who'd be starting rows and that stuff. They reckon he'd been keeping an eye out for the Prods. That was the joke going round. There'll be payback for that, so there will. That's just the way it is up there. You're just waiting for the next hiding all the time.

So I seen that blonde thing, the wee one who was shouting and roaring on the street the night before. I was just going past the Credit Union or whatever it is and she was coming out. I tell you, she looked lovely. I slowed down, just to watch her a wee bit, pervy as fuck. She'd a black eye from that big fat fucker who hit her. And her wee nose looked like it had taken a punch as well. Her hair was all soaking wet, so it was. All stuck to her face. Her umbrella was knackered. Sad sight, like.

I thought then, holy fuck, she's only about sixteen. When she was all pissed the night before I thought she was about thirty or something. But she's actually only a teenager. Really nice too, I promise.

So anyway, there's a few wee lads I know to see called Seanie and Mal and some others. They're wee hoods, so they are, always knocking about, sniffing away at the glue and nicking cars and stoning ambulances and shite like that. You know the sort of thing. So this Seanie and Mal and some minging wee whore they know were just coming out of the newsagents. I fucken knew rightly they were going to say something to Wee Blondie, with her black eye and all that. They just knew she was an easy target.

Sure as shite, Seanie pushes her. Fucken wee bastard. The poor girl, like. The three wee spides were laughing their heads off, probably on the glue. Just laughing away at her black eye and shouting 'Panda' and shite like that, all round her. Wee Blondie pulled away, all flustered and red and her umbrella all knackered and everything, and off she went. It wasn't much to be honest, but on top of all the bollocks she'd been going through, I'd say she was just about as unhappy as she could be at that moment. I know she wasn't dying or anything mad like that, but she probably wished she fucken was.

A while later I'd about four big whiskies and a couple

of beers in me and I was feeling sound as a pound, so I was. I never like drinking too much before working the next day, so I had this way of doing it quickly and early so I'd get a decent kip and not wake up all fucken blocked all over the place. I wouldn't have been drinking every night like, just now and then. Always Mondays and Tuesdays, then maybe about Friday and Saturday again. That's not totally accurate, but you know what I mean. Sunday afternoons can be good sometimes too. But I didn't really have any drinking buddies or anything. I was fucked off with the whole friendship thing, to be honest with you. I'd just been avoiding it.

So there was this bollocks on telly about how fucked the peace process is. BBC Northern Ireland stuff. Some cunt putting questions to the usual panel of dizzy bastards who go gurning about everyone being shite except themselves. The way they stack the panel – one Prod, one Catholic, one Prod, one Catholic – always makes me smile. It's so fucken sad, like. It shows how low this place has gone that they have to do that. They're just spoon-feeding the fucken losers who watch the thing. If it wasn't that way, people would be on the phone complaining, so they would. They'd be on saying 'oh there was too many Taigs on that' or 'why didn't you let more Catholics speak?' and all that oul bollocks. And in the audience the same stupid fuckers are always sitting there, jumping up and down with their arms in the air, waiting to tell someone on the panel he's a cunt. You always see them on these shows, the same faces. It's like they go on and try and say they're the normal people, but they haven't a clue about this town. They just hide in wee caves so they do. There's dead-on people in Belfast, but then when there's some TV show they vanish and the wankers are all over the screen talking all the usual talk, getting all pumped up and acting like they know everything. Television isn't in touch with the real world at all, I reckon. It just brings out all the wankers of the day, and they're only in it for themselves. To be honest, I often get riled up just watching it. What can you learn from TV? Fuck all, that's what.

So there's me, drinking drinks I hate the taste of, wearing a wet boiler suit, smelling of upholstery cleaner from the cars and cursing at the fucken telly. You'd swear I was about ninety. I'd been doing too much of that, I reckon. It'll be on me gravestone. 'He was an oul cunt of ninety when he was twenty-five.' Waste of time that'd be. You have to live, I swear. When it hits you, you know that you just have to get up and live.

Anyway, I was watching that and then that phone rang, the fancy wee mobile I'd nicked from over the road. Totally forgot about the thing, with all the work and the Arab and drink and rain and shite. So it was ringing away, some fucked-up loyalist ringtone, and I sat looking at it. It said on the wee screen that the caller was 'The Cunt'. That sounds like I made it up, now that I think of it, but honest, it said 'The Cunt'. Fuck it, I thought. So I answered it.

This guy goes: 'Tam?'

I'm like: 'No.'

And he's: 'Who's that?'

I says: 'Who's this?'

'It's The Count.' He said The Count. Then he says: 'Is Tam about?'

So I says: 'No.' And then I goes: 'The phone says The Cunt. Are you Cunt or Count?'

He goes: 'It's The Count. Fuck up. Where's Tam?'

I goes: 'He's at the shops.'

Your man goes: 'Tell him I'm looking him. I'm The Count, right?'

'Right. The Count, not The Cunt.'

'Right.'

And that was it. So do you reckon I gave Tam the message or what? Aye, right. For starters I didn't know who any of these fuckers were. Tam was probably the fat shite who battered Wee Blondie, but I hadn't a clue who The Cunt was. Or The Count. Here, that's my cue. Gotta go. Good luck to you.

Well, tough guy. Have a good weekend? I hope you didn't. I hope it was shite. At least I don't have to listen to you whingeing about it, if it was.

So you fed up listening yet? Well, don't worry, big lad, you can have next week off. Go on, I allow you. I promise not to do anything mad or nothing. I'll be sitting right here next Monday, good as wee shiny gold. Honest to fuck. You can trust me, so you can.

So I had to laugh this morning. The people in this place are so fucken sensitive, so they are. You wouldn't believe the bollocks I've had to listen to today, about being a bad employee and all. I don't want to get into it, so I don't. I'm not going to let it bother me. Ack sure I'll tell you later. Don't worry about it. It's nothing. It's nothing to me now, anyway.

So where were we? I was rabbiting away on Friday. Oh aye, I was saying about the phone and all that bollocks. Don't you worry, I never forget a word. Remember everything, me. It's a pain in the arse sometimes.

Anyway, I have to tell you this. The Cunt had rang me, right? Well, he rang Tam but he got me. The next day I was working again. That wasn't a bad day, to be honest. It wasn't wet and no one annoyed me in work. Karim was in great form and the other lads were a bit more lively than usual. A bunch of them had gone over to Scotland for the weekend and they'd been drinking the town dry. Old

Firm game in Glasgow, you know. So they were hungover as fuck, but happy as the people of Happytown, so they were.

You'll know them. Well, you might and you might not. As far as I'm concerned, they're this bunch of planks who think they're a bit clever, like. One of them calls himself Beezer, but when he first started here a year ago he was called Ronald. I call him Ronnie and he's always saying I should call him Beezer. So I asked him one day why the fuck should I call him Beezer? If it was a real nickname, fair enough. But because he just gave it to himself one day, it didn't count. You can't go round just changing your name and calling yourself whatever the fuck you want. I'd change me name every day if that was how it worked, just to keep people guessing. But you have to earn a nick-name, I reckon. Mine used to be Sidewinder, so it did. I fucken hated that. So anyway, he's Ronnie to me, even though it annoys the bollocks off him. Do Ron Ron, like. Big Rangers man. Thick as the day he was conceived up his mother's arse, so he is.

Then there's that wanker Liam, who thinks he's L. He's big into his Celtic, so he is. Nosey bastard. You'd get on well with him. His Da was shot dead by loyalists when he was a wee lad. He saw it happen and all, and he won't stop going on about it. Who gives a fuck, like?

Then there's Ian, who goes round saying he's Creamer. Something to do with the amount of women he claims he's screwing. He's virgin as fuck, so he is. Karim asked him where the clit was one day and he said it was between the fanny and the arse. Fuck's sake. Oul Ian must be down there licking away some nights and God knows what the poor girl's thinking. He's a Prod too. Plays the flute in a band up the Newtownards Road somewhere.

Says he had a brother kicked to death by Taigs one night. Boo fucken hoo. It's like you need a death in the family to work round here. And they never stop going on about it. They love to gurn about their misery, so they do.

And then there's Hugh, who's sort of dead polite and courteous and all. Half his family are supposed to be in the IRA. He reads loads and all, but he can't see a fucken thing without his glasses. I'm always nicking them from him and he's left half blind.

Then there's Karim, he's the Arab, and Steven. You must know Steven, if you know any of them. He's the English dick in the suit who comes in and out of the place giving orders. We don't know what he does except tell us what to do and sit in his wee office. He can never even look you in the eye if he's asking you to do something. He told me one day he was from Shropshire. I call it Shropshite and it annoys the fuck out of him. I'm always saying 'how's Shropshite' and he clenches his fists and all. He's a cunt, so he is. Steven doesn't have a nickname. Not one that I know of. Unless his real name's Cecil or something.

So there's six of us on the Car Wash, and Steve the Co-ordinator. But it's like them TV panels, so it is. Two Prods and two Taigs and the Arab. A wee balanced unit. It's pathetic. It annoys my head. And then there's me, Fletcher the Freak. You know me. I don't know if you can see me, but I'm the wee skinny, malnourished-looking bollocks. I sit in the big red chair in the kitchen, so I do. Usually covered in dirt. You probably know all this oul fanny anyway, but I'm just having a bit of a chat. Go easy on me.

So we do the insides and the outsides of the motors. And by the way, write this down. We graft all day long, like no other cunt in these buildings. We're underground all fucken day with hardly any natural light, so we are. No other bastard on the whole Stormont Estate has to put up with that. And you should know as well that we keep everything we find in the cars, and fuck you if it makes you cry. Finders keepers.

Ian's here the longest. He thinks he's a bit of a boss after Steven, but he can't really cut it with the likes of me and the Arab around. He's got no title or nothing but wishes he did. When I started here he gave me a few orders and shite but that soon stopped, I promise you. I reckon he never got the hang of me. He couldn't suss me out so he doesn't know how to get at me. He's bigger than me and all, because I'm not a big bastard. But he has a wee timid streak in him. The Arab's the only one I ever met here who wasn't full of the usual Northern Ireland bollocks. And, I promise you, no one ever gave an order to Karim. The only one who did that is the God of Muslims. Fucken Mohammed or Allah or whoever. And fair play to him. No one ever stood up to Karim except me.

So, aye. I told myself not to get any booze on the way home. I still had plenty left in that shitty whiskey bottle and I'd a couple of those Belgian piss samples left too. So I kept that in mind going past the offie and that was grand. I'd got a pizza and some garlic bread and I was just going to roast the fuck out of those for me tea, and that would do me the best. A wee Italian meal. Lovely. I was sort of treating myself, just for the hell of it. I remember I was even going to have a wee wank when I got in, after I'd had me scran and cracked open a fresh bottle of Belgian's piss. A wee one-man wanking party, like. Sure we all do it. Write it down to fuck. I've nothing to hide.

To be honest, I'd been thinking a bit about Wee Blondie and her being all blocked the other night. Wee chancy thing like that, eh? Knickers would be down round her ankles in no time, so they would. Anyway it wasn't long before I was thinking about her again, and looking out the window of me pokey wee flat to see if she was about the place. They'd got that wee window in the door fixed, the one she broke the other night. So I thought maybe it was all happy families again in the fucked-up house over the street.

Then I seen that wee fucker Seanie and that silly ugly wee bitch he hangs round with. The two of them were sniffing away at the glue. They'd sort of spilled out of the end of the alleyway behind Wee Blondie's house. They're always in there drinking and fingering and sticking fireworks up cats' holes and stuff. They weren't laughing or nothing, just trying to stand up straight and staring into space and all. That fucken glue is mental. It rots the brain, so it does. Although not quick enough. Any cunt who does that shite deserves to die. All right, I did it myself a wee bit, but you know what I mean.

So then I thought, fuck this. I put on me shoes and coat and ducked out of the flat and down the stairway. I sort of ran over the road and behind the houses, half keeping me head down, as if that would make me fucken invisible. Master of disguise or what? So I went up into the other end of the alley. The two wee wankers were standing down at the bottom still sucking away at the gluebags like it was mother's milk. They were moaning and all, wasted to fuck, half sort of laughing but not even able to move their jaws. They sounded like oul cows or something.

I gave them some fucken shock, I promise you. I came up on them fast, out of nowhere. They both looked at me, but they didn't have a clue what they were seeing. They couldn't focus or nothing. Glueheads have no idea what's going on at the best of times. I grabbed an ear on both of their wee fucken heads. I squeezed them dead tight, like. I'd a real good grip on them. They were just staring at me, trying to work out what the fuck was going on. Their faces were sort of crumpling up a wee bit with the pain. Seanie dropped his gluebag and tried to grab at me. Even if he'd got me arm, he'd no strength anyway. I just held the ears tight and brought their dirty wee heads in close together. I just cracked them dead hard like a couple of them cymbals. The noise was great. It was like I'd dropped a brick on the street or something. She started wriggling her dirty wee fingers and screaming and all, sort of grabbing all round her. Wee Seanie tried to grab me again and I pushed him back against the wall. I took the back of the bitch's head and rammed her face into the wall beside him. It got her right on her fat wee nose. So I did it again, turning her face round a bit so I cracked the side of her head. She just dropped down then. Her legs went all jelly and she just hit the deck.

Seanie was sort of pushing himself off the wall, trying to speak. His mouth all mangling the words. There was oul slabber and spit dripping off his lips. I punched him straight on the face – a real hard fucken blow. His wee head just thumped back against the wall. Then his legs gave way too and he fell on his arse. Then I hit him a sharp wee kick in the face. Two wee fucken nosebleeds. Then I thought fuck it and went for the pockets, them moaning away. They'd fuck all on them except two tubes of glue. Nothing else. No keys or money or nothing. I squeezed a bit of glue out of the top of the tube and into Seanie's face. I just pushed his head back against the wall and smeared the cunt with it. I held his eyelid open and poured it in there as well, sticking the fucken nozzle into his eyeball. It was flickering away like fuck. He was trying to close it, but he hadn't a hope. His hands and his head were shaking and all. He was fucked. I was standing there doing that and some fucker walked up the alley behind me. But he just went on ahead, smoking his fag and arguing with himself. He didn't even look back. Seanie was rubbing away at his eye. He didn't know what the fuck had got into it. You should have seen the two of them there, half propped up against the wall like two zombies. Two wee zombies in love. Sweet, eh? I know, I'm breaking your heart here.

Anyway, fuck's sake. I might have known that the pizza was burned black by the time I got back. So much for me Italian cooking, know what I mean? So I just whacked it out and started eating the bastard anyway. It near broke me teeth, so it did. Me hands were covered in glue and dirt and shite, but I just chewed away anyway. I was starving and I didn't care one wee bit. I'll probably get one of them diseases.

So I watched out on the street just to see what happened with Seanie and the ugly bitch, but they didn't show at all. I was mostly looking to see if Wee Blondie was going to show again. I don't know if her and fat Tam had fucked off after the row, or if he'd thrown her out of the house or what. I reckoned then that she might be his daughter. He'd be old enough to be her Da anyway. But I didn't know. Sure you wouldn't know what's going on in some mad wee house like that.

Here, there's Steven. Hang on. I'm going to tell him to fuck off. Might as well.

D6–14. March 15. Monday.
14.31
Speaker(s): Woundlicker

Well, mucker? How goes it? Big Ronnie's got a bottle of
tequila with him there. His girlfriend was away on some
holiday in Benidorm. She came back with a big pile of
cheap drink, so she did. Check that out if you want
something to do. Report it or something. I don't give a
shite. He's giving out wee shots of it. It puts the head
away, that stuff. I'd a wee bit there and I'm feeling the
better for it, I tell you. He didn't want to give me any, but
what could he do? I'd get you some too only you're a
cunt, so you are. Ack you're all right really. Bit quiet.

Cactus juice, so it is. Tequila. That's what it says on the
bottle, anyway. Just what you'd need if you were stuck in
the desert too. Mother Nature's a star, eh?

So here, your man Tam, right? I was telling you about
him before. I knew for sure he was involved. I'd seen him
from me window with three different cars in one week
last summer, and he's not a chauffeur or nothing. So that
means to me that he must have been at the moving end of
things, shipping drugs or guns or some shit about the
place. He was always around, so he was. That summer he
stood up at the end of the street every fucken day. Even
when the shite was hitting the fan with the marches and
riots and all, he'd just be standing there, up with the
loyalists, scratching his fat arse, and talking on his phone,
all innocent. But he was organising something. You can
just tell by the look of him, you can tell he's a fucken

player, like. You can tell by the way he walks. I could spot
a player, loyalist or republican, anywhere. I could spot him
coming down the street and tell you what side he was on.
It's all in the clothes and the shoes and the jewellery and
the haircut and all. Trained eyes can see shite coming a
mile off. Tam couldn't have looked more like a fat loyalist
bastard if he tried. Probably poured about twenty pints
into him for Ulster every night, the dickhead.

I mean, do you know how much the players run the
place round there? It's a joke. They're at this community
development bullshit now, instead of shooting up the
place. Community development, fuck's sake. That always
makes me laugh. They were doing community
development when they were chucking bottles of piss at
Fenian schoolgirls. Community development's all about
hiding guns and stoning pensioners, so it is. And riots are
community development as well.

I remember in Ardoyne years ago when the Taigs used to
get wee lads to run down the street shouting at everyone to
open their doors, so I do. Then when the shit kicked off,
the rioters would chuck the petrol bombs and then just run
in and out through the front and backs of houses, just
vanishing into wee holes. Peelers couldn't keep track of
fuck all, so they couldn't.

Me Da fucken hated being told to do that – to keep his
door open and all. He got so much shit from them the
rest of the time that he hated having to take their orders.
But when he said no, they just came and kicked the
fucken door in anyway and used the house. Then they'd
kick the fuck out of him later on. The laugh was that then
Sinn Féin would blame the Peelers for the damage to the
door and me Da would be told to claim the cops busted it
and talk to the papers about police violence and all. It was

either that or maybe me or me Ma would get a hiding on the street. Sometimes it was both. Pain in the arse, so it was.

Now the same wee fuckers are older and just walking into people's houses all the time, setting up wee robberies, keeping their hands in and running drugs and guns and shite like that. They just use people, so they do. There's nothing you can do to stop them. Dirty parasites, that's what they are. I hate all the paramilitaries – INLA, UDA, IRA or whatever. They're just wee parasites living off the backs of the people.

Right, let me explain this here. I've got the picture in me head and I know how to explain it to you, so I do. It's probably Ronnie's cactus juice talking here. Imagine there's a big capital T, right? A big giant one. I live sort of where the top of the T joins the rest of it. Know what I mean? So if I look out me window, I see down the length of the Peaceline. It runs out in front of me, into the distance. It would come further and run all the way through my building only there's the main road below me window. The main road makes the top of the T. They're going to close that off one day and knock down the flats where I live and bring the Peaceline on through, they reckon. But as it is, from me window, you can see republican homes on the left of the Peaceline and loyalists on the right. There's a big red iron gate on the main road, just below me, beside Wee Blondie's. The Peelers close it off when there's a riot or whatever to keep people apart. But there's eight houses running along on that bit of the main street. Wee Blondie lives in one of those, her back wall more or less to the Peaceline. They're going to demolish those houses too. They would've done it already but there's still people living in them and they're not moving out unless the government gives them a fortune to do it. You have to use what you've got, I suppose. But then you see cunts like Tam end up owning one of the houses and he's one man who doesn't deserve anything. They already knocked down all the houses behind those ones and the Army fed the Peaceline up through, but the ones in the eight houses aren't moving yet.

See those houses? Some are Taigs and some are Prods, but because they're on the main road and everyone uses it, they're not really in the line of fire. Most of the windows are all barred and all, but the real shite goes on further back, on either side of the Peaceline, where you know for a fact what sort of area you're in.

There was a wee man once with a shop further on up the street below me. He got fucked big time by the protection rackets. The bastards came at him from all sides, so they did. The loys moved in first, then the republicans, all looking about a hundred quid a month. The republicans backed off because the loys had beaten them to it. They don't get in the way of each other's business, like. But your man couldn't pay. It was a wee sweet shop, fuck's sake. He'd got this government grant to set up the trade because no one else would do it. He reckoned he'd sell fags and sweets and toilet roll and stuff like that because you couldn't get that without going up the front, to the shops at the Crumlin Road. And at that time the front was like fucken Star Wars. There was trouble all the time.

So your man thought he'd do a bit of business further back, serving everyone and anyone, just to meet the need. But they came at him dead hard, so they did. It was only a couple of months before he was struggling to pay the fuckers. Then he got his last warning and one night they just burned the place to the ground. They robbed it clean first, then they burned it to fuck. Then they came after him for the insurance. Your man told them he didn't have any. No fucker could get insurance round here. He was trying to get it through some government scheme, but he didn't have it. They pushed like fuck for it anyway. It drove him mad as a bastard. He couldn't pay it in the end, so he got a good hiding one night and was put out of the area. He had a wee wife and a couple of kids too. They lived just behind me, so they did. As soon as your man got out of hospital he just packed his family up and went away to fuck. He was in a wheelchair then because of that beating. Crippled for life, so he was. I never seen him since. No one did. Wee Indian man, so he was. Maybe he went back to India or some place like that.

Holy fuck. That cunt's got another bottle of tequila. Wait till you see Fletcher the Scrounger operate here. I'll be fucken blocked by the end of this day with any luck.

So aye, I was saying something to you. What the fuck was
it? Me head's away here. Ronnie's fucken blocked. You
wanna see him. He reckons he's got a job in some garage
his mate runs or something. Bit of a mechanic, our
Ronnie. Beezer, like. We're all supposed to know about
cars and all, but we spend most of the time just washing
them. There's a mechanic comes round every now and
then to go over them and all, but we're supposed to keep
them in good running order. No one bothers their arse.
But see Ronnie? He'd fucken kill to get out of this place
and get working on cars, so he would.

So listen. I drank some of that oul whiskey that night.
To be honest, I was thinking about having a bit of a wank
again. I don't mind telling you, mate. The way I do it,
right, I like to build up to it. I keep it in the mind and
plan it out a wee bit. It's like having a dirty love life and
waiting to meet her in your own bed, so it is. But my love
life was down the fucken spout so the oul hand was
having to do the trick. And I enjoyed it too. I don't mind
the odd ham shank. It's just getting the right time and
right pictures in your mind and all. When it all falls into
place, it's as good as the real thing. Cheapest high you can
get, so it is. Free, like.

I was thinking I'd like to see Blondie again before I did
it. A wee smasher, so she is. Never fucken laid eyes on her
before all that, but she's a wee cracker. Tits pointing out at

you, big dark eyes looking straight ahead. She's like in her own world, on her own road. Crazy-looking wee thing. Wee high cheeks on her. Kind of innocent face, but you know rightly she's been in the saddle more times than John fucken Wayne. So I didn't pull me wire. I refrained, as they say in England. I just put it out of me head and got on with doing fuck all squared instead. I'd wait until I got a look at her again. I didn't have enough dirt to go on. Know what I mean? I'd wait to get another look at her legs or her wee tight arse. Sweet anticipation. Makes it all the better, eh?

Then some Cockney fucker on the telly started a fight with some slapper in this doctor's office and she threw a phone at him. It hit him on the head, so it did. I saw that and laughed. Laugh or cry, that's me. It's mad sometimes. I laughed like a fucken madman, so I did. It wasn't even funny. Then I thought fuck it, what about that wee mobile? I'd turned the thing off after your man The Cunt rang, so I had. I didn't know what else to do. The battery would be running out and I wanted to keep the thing powered a wee bit longer.

So I switched it on then. There were a few beeps and the thing said there were three texts. One was from 'The Cunt'. It said 'Ring me'. Then there was another one from some other number that said 'You'll be found'. And then there was one other wee one from 'Molly' saying 'Not coming back. Fuck you.' So what the fuck was oul Fletcher supposed to do?

Number one, from The Cunt. I texted him back and said 'Fuck off you're a Cunt'. That made me laugh, but maybe he got that sort of shite all the time. Then the second one – I wrote back and said 'You couldn't find your hole with your hands tied behind your back'. I laughed again at that. And then the third one – I reckoned this Molly one might've been Wee Blondie. I didn't know, but I rang it anyway.

She goes: 'Tam? What the fuck do you want?'

I'm like: 'Hello. How are you?'

So she says: 'Who's this?'

So I goes: 'Who's this?'

She's all: 'Here, are you the one stole Tam's phone?'

I says: 'Might be.'

'He's going to fucken kill you.'

I'm like: 'Aye right.'

She's like: 'He fucken is. I swear.'

So I says: 'From his hospital bed?'

She goes: 'What?'

I laughed, like. Then I says: 'He can't kill me if he's in hospital with three broken legs and four broken arms and a busted head and shite.'

She's all: 'Is he in hospital?'

I goes: 'Not yet, honey bun.'

Then she's all: 'Who the fuck are you?'

I just says: 'I'm a friend. Do you want Tam to go into hospital?'

'You taking the piss out of me?'

'No. It's a simple question, love. What time do you want him to go in at?'

'What do you mean?'

'You know what I mean. I'll arrange it. He's a bad cunt, so he is.'

She goes: 'Who the fuck's this?'

I went on anyway: 'I know he hit a girl at his house the other night. It was you, wasn't it?'

'How do you know that?'

'I know lots of things.'

'You spying on me or something?'

'No. You just walked past me one day and made me heart bounce.'

She goes: 'Right. Thanks. Are you going to hurt him?'

'Aye. And why not?'

'Fuck.'

'Well?'

'You're mad, so you are.'

'Aye. Mad about you.' Then I goes: 'So what age are you?'

She says: 'I'm seventeen. What age are you?'

'Twenty-five.' Then I goes: 'Twenty-five and half alive. So are you called Molly?'

'Aye. Who are you?'

'Fletcher.'

'Hello Fletcher.'

'Hello Molly.'

She goes: 'I'm going to tell Tam you rang.'

I'm like: 'Go on ahead. Tell the fat fuck to keep his eyes peeled, right? Fletcher the Fucker's on the loose.'

'You think you're fucken funny?'

'Aye. Hilarious.'

'Right. Okay. I better go.'

'Fair enough. Short and sweet. Just like you. Nice chatting.'

'Aye, you too. I never spoke to a psycho before.'

I laughed and says: 'I wouldn't be so sure about that, Molly.'

'Aye. Cheerio.'

'Cheerio.'

And that was about it, mate. Not much of a conversation, but it tickled me in the right places, I promise you. I never asked her who your man Tam was to her, but I reckoned he was riding her all right. Who the fuck wouldn't?

I loved the way she spoke though. The way she said 'Hello Fletcher' was dead nice. And the way she said 'Cheerio'. It was like a wee breath. It even sounded like a wee flirt. Then the phone rang. It was The Cunt. I hadn't a fucken clue what to say to the wanker, but I answered anyway.

I goes: 'Hello?'

He says: 'Fuck you, Tam. The fucken deal's off, you stupid cunt. What kind of shite are you playing at?'

I went: 'Fuck off.'

And he hung up. So that was that one, whatever that was. But the other one never got back. Tam, I think. The bastard who said he'd find me. I left the phone switched on after that. I just wanted to see who was going to threaten me and all. Sure, they hadn't a clue who I was.

Wee honey, our Molly. Just like a wee Cameron Diaz. Here, I'm away for a piss.

Hello, fuckhead. Good evening to you, Mister Bond. You have ways of making me talk, you know? You shall extract my full confession with your ingenious plan to loosen my jaw. Or I could just make it easier, eh? Aye. We'll do that. I'll spill the beans and you eat them up. Any crack with you anyway? Nah, didn't fucken think so, you boring bastard. You'd need a pacemaker round here. Me heart could give out with the excitement of talking to you.

Smell that, big lad. Can you smell me breath through that thing? Rank, mate. Stinking, like. I smell like a wino. So Steven tells me anyway, the boring bastard. At least I don't smell like I wear perfume, I said to him. I smell like a wino who's lost in the desert, I told him. He thinks I'm nuts sometimes.

So right anyway, the next bit of the story. You'll need to know all this stuff, big lad. It was, fuck I don't know, Thursday or something. Thursday, aye. Karim was going bonkers in work. A Man from England had come over to do something or other and half the Northern Ireland Office were running round with their arses on fire. So that meant cars. Armour-plated cars, staff cars, special cars, the works.

That's what they were to us, these top fuckers. Mandarins, they call them. Or ministers, sometimes. Whatever. Important people, anyway. Supposedly. They were just Men from England to us. You might catch sight of one of them when you took a car out to meet a driver at Parliament Buildings or somewhere, but they looked like fuck all to me. I never knew who they were. They'd be all protected by men in suits, in case some fucker took a rattle at them. But they'd just look depressed the whole time. To be honest, you'd be doing well to look happy in this town when there's loads of people here who'd love to kill you.

Anyway, we had to put thirty-one cars out by eleven in the morning. Thirty fucken one. More than ever before, so it was. That meant checking all the clean ones that were ordered, and cleaning the dirty ones that had just been left back. And when there's a Man from England about, it has to be done right. I tell you, we worked our fingers to the bone.

Oul Karim had been up all night because of some oul dog barking out a back street where he lives. Up the Ormeau or somewhere like that. He'd gone out about four in the morning looking to kill the yappy bastard, but he couldn't track it down. He was ripping about being kept awake, so he was. His eyes were all bloodshot and his skin had gone all blotchy and shite. It was mad as fuck to see him when he hadn't had a good kip. It upset him, big time. I was laughing away. Anyway, then he finds there's a Man from England who needs thirty-one fucken cars and he's even more ripping. There was chat then that it might be the Prime Minister, but we didn't know. They never tell us anything. We'd see it later on the news if it was. To be honest, I couldn't give a fuck. All I was thinking about was if they were going to dirty up the cars or not. If they did, that would wreck the rest of the week too, when they were all brought back. Fuck's sake.

We got the motors all out by about ten past eleven and got the thumbs up from some wanker who came running in to get the last car. He'd a pinstripe suit, briefcase, sunglasses and whatnot. Karim gave him the fingers, and your man pretended not to notice. He just goes 'Cheers, lads'. He was from London or somewhere. I laughed and went up the back steps with the Arab for a bit of fresh air.

There's sort of a patch of waste ground with tufts of grass and weeds and that growing out the back. And there's a big wire fence a bit further along, where the birds sit and shite all round the place. Me and your man just sat there, not saying much, looking at these pigeons, or whatever the fuck they were.

So Karim broke out the grass, as per usual, and I had a wee toke of a joint. It wiped me out a wee bit, I tell you. He smokes this African weed shit that's dead strong. It's some mad stuff some mate of his posts him over from Holland. So that's why I just sat there saying nothing, grinning like an eejit and staring at the fucken fence. Leave no turn unstoned, that's my motto. I know, sponging again. What can I do, like? I'm not going to go buying anything from the cunts round my way. That's just feeding the paramilitaries, so it is.

So oul Karim was pissed off again. Real shite mood, like. He started giving out about the NIO, saying they were trying to keep people down and all this. He was just tired, maybe. But it's a load of bollocks. I mean, the guy would always go on about how he hates everyone, even the Northern Irish people who he thinks are so oppressed by the British government. I tried to tell him to come and look at who's oppressing people round my way, but he wouldn't listen.

I asked him then why he gives a fuck, if he thinks everyone from Northern Ireland is a bastard anyway. He said it was part of the Western system that had fucked everyone up and we didn't know how much we were being manipulated and all this. Prods and Taigs, all being shafted by the same system. Divide and conquer and all that. It sounds wise when you're stoned, but I like to keep me wits about me. I have to say that no one could talk shite like that guy. To make that fucker happy you'd have had to close down all the pubs and kill everyone who didn't face the petrol pump and pray on their wee mat five times every day. What the fuck, like?

So after a bit longer, and for the millionth time, I told him he was totally fucked up in his wee beardie head. I told him the Arabs were wankers and all the usual shite. That drove him crackers. He says I could go somewhere else for a smoke in future. I told the cunt to get out of my country and we stared at each other and thought about killing each other and all. But it's just a laugh, though. Sometimes I wanted to just do something mad to the fucker, like skinning his oul brown skin off and throwing him in a barrel of salt, or chopping his head off or some shite. But the rest of the time I just had a laugh. I couldn't give a fuck about Northern Ireland anyway. I'm not going to stand round defending the place. Why people get so uptight about it is way over my head. Know what I mean? Karim was right in one way. The place is fucked.

So anyway. What was it? Aye, me and him made up after looking at the birds sitting on the fence. I don't know how that worked, but the African weed had a lot to do with it. It was dead on to just look at them sitting there, shitting and cooing all over the place, and wondering what they were thinking about.

He had the idea to head out after work for a few pints. Fine by me, I says. The only thing was that the wanker wouldn't touch a drop. He was dead strict about that, but it was fine by me all the same. I mean, who am I to turn down a social life, like? Billy-fucken-no-mates, me.

We got away a wee bit early because of the day that was in it. We all fucked off after four instead of the usual half five or six. We'd all agreed to come in on the Saturday anyway, to sort all the extra cars out when they were finally brought back. But it was cleared with Steven to go, so it's not like we all just vanished. There's no real rebels where I work. They're all arse-lickers. I'm not one of them.

So as it turned out, me and Karim got a lift into town with Steven. When it's out of working hours, I swear he always goes on about shagging one-night stands the whole time. He's so full of shite, it's unbelievable. I think he just tries to impress us or something. But oul Karim loved to hear about any dirty oul fucker doing anything with a woman. He knew Steven was as full of shite as I did, but he still loved the stories. You just had to say the word 'cunt' to Karim and his eyes would light up, the dirty bastard. And he'd have heard that word a lot in his life in Belfast, so he would.

So your man Steven told us this oul bollocks about going to some club the weekend before and going home after it with two lesbians. He says he shagged them both and then they did a lesbo show for him after and all. For fuck's sake. It was the worst made-up story I've ever heard. I mean, as if. Too much porn, not enough porking for that fella I'd say.

So here's us, me and the Arab, dropped off in the middle of Belfast, wearing our boiler suits, stinking like fuck, knackered and half-stoned. We could have taken showers back at Stormont but we'd have had nothing to change into afterwards anyway. Fuck it.

At that time of day most of the pubs have loads of suits and that lot in them, but we didn't give a shite. We went into this bar on May Street for a pint. Well I had a pint, the Arab had an orange juice. The same man would murder a million Jews and smoke more dope than you could carry, but he'd go nuts if you tried to tell him to have a pint. Mad as fuck, like.

I was thinking in there, in that pub, how I must be about the same age as most of the suits. They'd all look down on me because of what I'm wearing. It's like they expect me to be more like them. I don't know why they would think that. To be honest, it used to annoy me, but I don't care now. I never really had a career and I never will. Okay I've been flat broke me whole life, but I'd say I've been happy enough in the head and stuff, so who gives a fuck? I've still got me wits about me, you know. But some of these guys seemed to have a problem with me looking the way I did. I suppose smelling like shite and hanging round with a blotchy Arab fundamentalist doesn't help, but it was none of their business. I reckon sometimes they probably think 'where did it all go wrong?' when they look at me. I just think back 'how come your two front teeth are flying through the fucken air?'

So we went into about six pubs and people gave me and Karim the evil eye in every single fucken one of them. By the time we got to Lavery's Bar, I was a bit steaming and Karim was busting to get someone's vagina onto the end of his tongue. He'd been going on again about how pissed off he was and how he hated this country and the West and all. It was boring. But soon he was talking about all the women here being whores and all, and then, sure as fuck, he started on about sex. So by that time I was on about Arabs being crackers and he was on about these thongs he'd seen. The way he was going on about them, you'd swear he'd cut a hole in the mannequin he'd seen modelling them and ride it in the fucken shop.

So anyway, in Lavery's there was a wee bit of a problem. Some loyalist fuckwit with a chunky zero-carat gold chain round his neck told Karim there was another bar upstairs he might want to try. By the way he said it, I wasn't sure what he meant. But I reckon he was basically asking him to leave anyway, just because he's an Arab, like. Karim told him straight out that he'd bring him upstairs and throw him out the fucken window if he spoke to him again. Mad bastard, like. Your man just laughed and then looked away. I reckoned things could have got out of hand from there, but Karim wouldn't leave. He wouldn't move an inch to try and defuse the thing. So fuck it, I thought. He's just right. Don't let the bastards get you down.

So the Hun and his mate were drinking away and then another two came in and joined them. I was drinking shitty whiskey by that stage, pouring a wee drop of courage into me in case the thing blew up all over the fucken place. I'd started talking shite too, drunk as fuck, so I was. I was a bit loose at the mouth and I started saying to Karim about wee Molly. I told him I'd rang her and all and that we were getting on a bit. I'd swear she liked me a wee shade, just from that one phone call. But I didn't know for sure or anything.

Then Karim started asking all the fucken questions of the day. He wanted to know about the size of her tits, the shape of her arse and even what length I thought her tongue might be, the dirty oul fecker. I told him I reckoned she'd forgot to put her tits on the last time I seen her, and he looked disappointed. I told him tit size isn't that important and he sort of shrugged. Then he asked me about the length of her fingers and I swear I just stopped answering him. I didn't want her being violated by that looper, even in his own wee dirty mind.

It was mad because the four loyalists just totally fucken ignored us. Your man with the attitude must never have even mentioned what happened to the other fellas because they didn't even look our way at all. These are the same sort of headers who would kick the living fuck out of anyone if they took half a notion. But there was no sign of that coming at all. Not that I wanted it. I was just surprised it wasn't there, that's all.

In the next bar, The Empire, Karim started getting all wanky about the world again. It must have been all that fucken orange juice filling him up with acid or something, but he got all bitter and twisted. And I was wondering a wee bit if this was the dickhead's plan, to get me all hammered so he could just rant and fucken rave about the West and all when I was in no state to do anything except maybe fall over now and again. He might've just been looking for someone to spout at, I thought. Who would listen to his shite in Belfast except me? I'd felt a wee bit pissed off when he started all that stuff earlier, but I just accepted his way of going on. It doesn't really bother me when I think about it. Me Da told me one time there's an oul saying the Russians have where they go 'I drink and I drink and I am always drunk and there's nothing I am afraid of'. I felt like that. Just felt like saying fuck it all, fearing nothing and getting drunk. I don't know if the West is more fucked than the East or the South or whatever, but it's all a bit fucked.

And then I did a stupid thing. I shouldn't have done it, but I did it. I told him about that gun, you know the one? The pistol I'd picked up when I sneaked into Molly's house? Tam's pistol. Karim was dead interested. He said we'd have to go and talk about it, so I finished up me whiskey and we did. I didn't want to but I did. I knew this was a bad road to go down, but I couldn't just not talk about it now I'd said it. All of a sudden it sounded like a big thing. Fuck it. I went on outside anyway and we walked down the street, me drunk as a skunk, staggering all over the show.

Right. His thing was that if I'd got the gun and no one had seen me, then it was clean. It wouldn't matter what it had been used for before because no one knew who had it now. If the Peelers had forensics on it then your man Tam would be the suspect for using it, and then when they found out it had vanished from his house, it'd be anyone's guess. All of this was clever, all good points. But, as I told him, it only made sense if you're planning to use it. And if that's the deal, then the plan was probably to kill someone. I said I wasn't planning on killing anyone.

He goes: 'Not you, Fletcher, you fucking idiot.' His breath was rank as fuck, so it was. 'Me.'

So what was I to do? Not give the fucker the gun that I didn't really want anyway? Not give him it in case the mad Arab bastard went and killed someone? I knew that if I didn't give it to him he'd become the biggest bastard ever to work with. And what did I care anyway? I told him I'd sleep on the idea and talk to him in the morning. He told me he wanted the gun. I asked him who he wanted to kill, and he just smiled. He said the less I knew about it the better. He was probably right. To be honest, I was thinking that as long as it wasn't me or Wee Blondie, I couldn't give a flying fuck. He could even shoot himself if he wanted.

We went for one last wee jar at the top of Botanic in some joint called Renshaws. It was fucken full of Taigs going loopy about an Ireland match that had just finished. Half of them were in their green hoop Celtic shirts and the other half in Ireland tops, all standing round talking bollocks about the game. They were all pissed as cunts. I thought fuck it, we'll have another jar anyway. I got them in – an orange and a Powers – and downed mine. But then I seen Karim holding out his glass for me to say cheers. So I got a refill and said 'cheers'. He says 'To Allah – it's no finish,' and then he laughed, the creepy bastard. But I said the same thing and downed it.

Some big drunk cunt from Armagh or some country hole like that then said to me 'It's *sláinte.*' You know, Irish for cheers? As if me and Karim had been talking to him. I told him to fuck off and Karim stepped right up into his face and told him he'd a gun in his pocket and he'd shoot him right there if he ever spoke to me again. Your man just sneered at the Arab and backed off and went over to his mates. None of them even looked round at us.

It was weird as fuck, that day. I swear we could have been kicked to death by any amount of republican fuckheads or loyalist wankers, but none of them were bothered. I thought then that maybe it was the blotchy Arab, that he was scaring the fuck out of people because he was different and Muslim and all. They couldn't get the measure of him, I reckon.

So after that I got a taxi and Karim just walked on his merry way. I could've bet you a tenner he was on his merry way to get a hooker or some shite like that. To be honest, I wouldn't ever get a hooker in Belfast. If I'd ever been anywhere else I might have. Some nice German thing or some sultry French lady, but not at home. The half of them work for the paramilitaries. And they're all dogs anyway. I've seen a few of them down by the BBC in the so-called Red Light area. No thanks, mate. But if you're some hornball Arab with half his teeth missing from the middle of fucken nowhere, maybe you'd see that as exotic and erotic and whatnot. I don't know. But I reckoned Karim wouldn't be long slabbering about it if he got his hole. He was usually honest like that there.

The taxi driver then started going on about the match and I told him that I couldn't give a fuck about it. He said he wasn't saying he was an Ireland supporter and that he might be a Northern Ireland supporter and all this fucken guess-the-religion bollocks, and I told him to shut the fuck up. Give us a break, like. The last thing you need after coming out of a pub full of wankers is to get into a car with one sitting there in the driving seat and have to pay him for his wisdom.

I was starving to death but I just went home anyway. I didn't even try to cook anything because I was too blocked. I've done that before and it was a total disaster.

I just got home and stuck on the radio and bopped about for a bit. I kind of fancied some blow to smoke but Karim had that with him. So then I thought I'd get a bunch of it off him for giving over the gun. Fair deal and all that. And then I took the gun out from the drawer in the bedroom and started waving it round like I was in the fucken IRA or something. I pointed it out the window, down at Molly and Tam's, and pretended to shoot the place up. It was mad. Fucken heavy, guns. They make you feel like you've really got something in your hand.

To be honest, I ended up putting it down and dropping me trousers instead. I remember thinking that I must have a wank because I'd been busting to cum for days and I was feeling a bit horny. I wished to fuck that Wee Blondie would come out of the house bollock naked or some shite. Or just open the curtain and show her tits or stick a dildo up her hole or some bollocks like that. You know what I mean? But she didn't have any idea who or where I was, so unless she was bonkers, that was never going to happen. So I just sat there on the sofa, dreaming to myself, dick in hand. Next thing, I was dead to the world. Anyway, here's to you mate. Here's to you. I've a life to lead, you know.

Top of the morning. It's fucken Saint Patrick's Day
tomorrow. Forgot all about the cunt. It's on the news, so it
is. All the politicians are heading out to America to lick
the President's arse. DUP and UUP and Sinn Féin and
SDLP and all the rest of them. Don't start me on those
wankers, fuck's sake. They go out armed with a bunch of
shamrocks to try and get the Yanks to listen to their
whingeing. They just dine out on whatever wee bits of
sympathy they can scrape up. They love all that, so they
do. And if there's trouble back home – and there's always
a bit on Saint Paddy's – it suits them down to the ground.
It gets them more sympathy.

America, listen up. Catch yourselves on. Don't listen to
the cunts. They're fleecing you and you're too fucken slow
to see it. I mean, could you be bothered with all that?
Bastards, so they are. The whole fucken lot of them. I hate
the politicians in this country, so I do. None of them take
any blame for the shite they cause. I hate them all. Don't
start me. Anyone who ever stood for election in Northern
Ireland is a bastard. And that's it.

Anyway, no one's coming into work in the morning.
We're all supposed to go out and get full and all but I'm
giving it a miss, so I am. Fuck all the rest of them and
everything else. I'll be here, big lad, don't you worry.

So I was telling you the last time about the wee session I
had with oul Karim. Fuck's sake, that was a heavy one. So I

went home anyway and then, at 2.03 in the morning, I
woke up. I'd got into bed somehow, even though I'd
crashed out on the sofa. It must have been when I went for
a piss or something and I just took a wrong turn. At least I
hadn't pissed all round the place or anything. But me
trousers were totally off and I just had a smelly T-shirt on. It
says 'I ran the Belfast Marathon' on it. And then on the
back it says 'Did I fuck'. It was a wee joke of Ronnie's last
year. He gave us all one at work. Anyway, I'd woke up and
to be honest, I felt like absolute shite.

There was a riot going on below, so there was. That's
what it sounded like anyway. So I went to look and sure
enough, it was a bit of a ding–dong. Cops and soldiers
were parked on the main road at the top of the street on
the republican side and the gate over to the loyalist side
was closed. About twenty Peelers, in the full gear, were
facing the rioters with their shields in their hands and all.
The rocks and half bricks and ball bearings from catapults
were pelting into them. Some of them were knocked back
with the force, so they were. The Army were beaming
lights down into this gang of mad Taigs from a helicopter.
There was maybe a hundred of them, scarves wrapped
round faces, mostly teenagers, all fired–up to fuck.

One fella turned up with a crate of bottles and started
feeding them out. They were sending them through to the
wee lads at the front. And then, after just a few seconds
they were away, flying through the air. You could see
them flashing in the big beams. A bunch of them smashed
down onto the shields. Liquid and chunks of glass were
splashing up all over the place. Acid bombs, I'd bet. Then
more soldiers popped up and worked their way forward to
let some of the Peelers get back for bandages and air and
all.

Then I seen the feeding again. The same guy, another crate of bottles. This time you could tell they were petrol bombs because of the wee rags sticking out the top. They were lit as they went through the crowd. They were fired up in the air the second they got to the front line. They were going way up and tumbling down onto the fuckers as fast as I've ever seen. Dead angry, like. And then the crack of three shots rang out, so it did. Bang, bang, bang. None of the Peelers or soldiers went down, but I'd say some Provie had taken a rattle at them.

The loyalists were massing up on the other side, so they were, all excited by the noise and trying to fuck bricks over the Peaceline. They didn't have a baldy clue what the hell was going on. You could see them standing around, busting for a fight with anyone, just as soon as they worked out what the fuck was going on. The paranoid fucks. They're always waiting to be out-bred in north Belfast, so they are. It's mad. They're always gurning that the Taigs are humping away from no age and dropping babies and getting houses. That's why the Prods always want to get stuck into them, so it is. Turf thing, you know. They should throw their rubber johnnies away. That'd make more sense, if you're into counting heads and all.

So I bet the UDA were ready then, dying to shoot some Taig who got anywhere near them. The last thing the Peelers needed was for the loys to get involved. They can only handle one side at a time, so they can. But when that gate's closed, the two are totally separated, so they are. Locked up tight. Parts of this city can be turned into prisons in seconds.

So the Taigs were putting the pressure on anyway. There must have been thirty or forty bricks in the air every second. The Peelers and Army kept pretending they were going to surge forward, sort of pretending to run but then backing off. It didn't make any fucken difference. It just looked stupid. Then an ambulance rolled in behind the cops. No siren, like. They didn't want to make a fucken racket in case they got some too. I seen some cop with blood streaming from her head, from under the helmet, being treated on the ground. Whatever that was, it must have been some fucken whack. The Fenians were shouting like fuck 'die you bitch' and 'black bastards' and all this. Every time they shouted 'black bastards', the loyalists went fucken bonkers, jumping up and down thinking they were being called names. Black bastards.

At the back of the Taigs I could make out your man, that Sinn Féin councillor. You see him around here all the time. Artie Callaghan, his name is. Artie Kill-A-Man Callaghan, the Prods call him. I hate that cunt. One time when I lived up west he came round with a bunch of hard lads demanding everyone get out to vote for the party and all. He got me on the street and asked what would I vote, so he did. I was about sixteen, like. Wee cheeky bastard, so I was. I told him I'd vote for the Monster Raving Loony Party, just to annoy him. He gave me this real dirty look, so he did. It was fucken stupid, so it was. I walked away then and they all just stared at me. We got all the windows in the house put in that night. Fuck's sake. I was living with Fenian foster parents then, and the next thing I'm getting their windows put in. First it was the stones, and then a fucken petrol bomb. The living room went on fire. Burned to bits, so it did. Near killed us all.

I bet Artie had said something to someone about me. Then about a week later, just before an election, I was given this almighty kicking on the way to school. I was called Sidewinder and a Brit-lover and all. They pulled me down this bank and ripped me shirt off, about five of them. Got a tooth knocked out and had me balls kicked to fuck. Artie came into school to preach Provo a while later and just smiled when he seen me, so he did. The cunt. I wasn't long in that school after that. This priest reckoned I'd be killed if I didn't get out to fuck. He said I'd to go and do some soul-searching and all. He said I'd disappointed some people. I told him he should do some soul-searching himself. He called me a 'wee cunt' then, so he did. Holy people annoy me, so they do. Wankers.

Sinn Féin workers are always about the place when there's a riot on. Especially Artie Kill-A-Man Callaghan. Him with his hundred teenagers doing his dirty work for him. His hands never get dirty, know what I mean? You'd swear one man can be smarter than a whole street of people sometimes.

So I just fucken stared at the cunt that night as one of his wee lads carried another crate of bottles past him. He looked up and we both sort of locked eyes. I stepped back from the window then, just for a wee second. I took off the T-shirt, got the pistol and turned on the big light in the room. I went back to the window, naked as the day I was born. Artie was still staring up at me. You could have seen me from anywhere, so you could. I pointed the pistol at him and made it look like I was pulling the trigger. I did that until the fucker stepped back and away into the dark. The bastard chickened out. I reckon nudity can be a bit of a weapon sometimes. I know he seen me.

I stood there for a wee bit anyway, just watching the whole scene. The hoods were tiring, you could tell, and more reinforcements were arriving for the cops and soldiers. They've always got the most manpower at the end of the day. But the Taigs had given them something to think about, just out of the blue. They'd flexed a wee bit of muscle, hoping everyone would take notice.

Then your man Tam showed up, right? He pulled up at his house from the loyalist end of the main road. He got out and walked right up to the front door and just sort of kicked it in anger. Then he got out his keys and opened it. I reckoned Wee Blondie might be in a bit of bother, but to be honest I didn't even know if she was still in there. The riot was still the loudest thing going on so if he'd been up for battering her, I wouldn't really have known. I swear to God, it sounds weird as shit but I felt like going down there and firing some bricks at his house. I'd love to have done that and then gone and bricked the fucken wee rioting bastards too. And the fucken cops and that councillor cunt Artie Callaghan as well. I might even have been pumped-up enough to get a brick all the way over the peaceline that night, and got the loys involved too. I swear, I could've leaned out that window and shot some bastard. Anyone out there at all.

I thought about Tam then. I could just imagine the bullet flying down in slow motion and smashing his fucken head open and ramming into his brain and ripping it up and tearing out the other side of his head and bringing wee bits of his fucken skull with it. I could see it all in me head. I had to breathe in deeply then and calm down before I lost the plot. It hit me that I was standing there bollock naked, thinking about Tam's brain flying out of his head. Mad.

Then I thought fuck it, I've to go to bed here. I was knackered anyway. I mean I'd been out drinking all night and here I was pissing about again. To be honest, I could've slept standing up. I looked over at Wee Blondie's and nothing was happening anyway. I mean, I didn't even know why I was wasting me time thinking about her. She was nice like, but not worth going insane in the brain for. I was having some kind of crush or fantasy about her and I'd only spoken to the bitch once. It must have been because of those two glueheads I fucked up. I mean, the only reason I did that was because of Wee Blondie. It was mad. I didn't even know who she was. I couldn't work it out. It was crazy. I think I was just horny and angry and it was just messing with me head. That's all it came down to. I just had this dose of the horn and it was like it was pointing in her direction. Girl next door thing. It just all seemed stupid.

So I went back to bed and lay there, listening to the thing die down outside and planning out this mighty wank to help me say cheerio to Wee Blondie. I reckoned if I just degraded her in me mind or something, then I'd get over it. Just turned her into a wee slapper, you know. Then didn't the fucken mobile ring? The one I'd nicked from your man Tam. The one I'd spoke to Wee Blondie on.

So she's like: 'Hello.' She's whispering away, dead quiet.

I goes: 'Hello.' I was whispering too. 'I was just thinking about you.'

She says: 'Yeah. Me too. So, Tam? Eight o'clock tomorrow night. Okay?'

I'm all: 'Shit. Okay. Where at?'

She says: 'He'll be meeting someone in the Cregagh Bucket at eight.'

So I goes: 'Right.'

She says: 'Right then, Fletcher?'

I says: 'Wee buns, love. Just you wait and see what I'll do for you, Molly.'

Then she goes: 'I'll be thinking of you. Cheerio.'

I said: 'Cheerio.'

And that was it. I mean, that was the end of the big
plan to wise up. But I swear, if you'd heard her speak
you'd know what was going through me head then. It was
like getting a call from a wee angel or something. It made
me heart beat like fuck. So what else could I do? I mean,
that's what you have to ask yourself. What the fuck was I
going to do? Well, I knew straight away. I was going to
sort this shite out. I was going to belt the bollocks off that
fucker Tam. Hospital job, just like I'd said. So that was that,
like.

And here, there's Ian. Big Creamer, the fantasy fuck of
every woman alive, like. Look at the swagger and the
sunglasses on him and it's the middle of March. No way.
You can tell he's the only man to ever discover the clit
isn't connected to the vagina. Look at the walk of him. He
hasn't a clue I'm sitting here watching. These blacked-out
windows are brilliant, so they are. You'll turn me into a
spy myself. Here, I'm away to jump out on the fucker and
nick his shades. Ruin his day. See you later.

All right, Brit? It's Fletcher Fee, diddly dee. Happy Saint
Paddy's Day. You're still there, aren't you? You haven't been
shot dead or blown up or any of that shite? Nah. I doubt
it. Northern Ireland's too sensible now, isn't it? Is it fuck.

I'm just in the door, so I am. I walked it up this
morning, just for the hell of it. Took me near three fucken
hours. That's why I'm only in. It's good to stretch the oul
legs. I don't take enough exercise, so I don't.

They're having a big parade up the town there. It's all
wee green babies and green beer and drunk spides and
republican T-shirts and all. Welcome to New York, fuck's
sake. In a few hours it'll basically be a bunch of drunk
bastards waving the Tricolour around past Prod areas, and
a bunch of drunk Prods waiting for any Taig to pass by. It's
easier not to even bother working out who's worse. Fuck
them all. You know, there's no celebrations in this town
that don't end up with a scrap. Same thing, to a lot of
people.

Anyway. Fuck it all. I doubt if Saint Patrick would
even go to Saint Patrick's Day here, so I do. He'd be
fucken better off in New York, so he would. Or at least
down South or somewhere, where it's not all about
politics and shite.

I'm here to see you today, you know that? I mean, I
don't have to be here, but I came in to sit on me arse and
talk to you anyway. Dedication, eh? Dedication to talking

to myself. First sign of madness, so it is. Talking to
yourself, like. The voices in me head just come straight out
me mouth, so they do.

I was telling you about the phone call from Wee
Blondie. You have to hear this. Write this down. This is
what I wanted to tell you. Right, I didn't chicken out in
the morning at all. I mean about giving the gun to Karim,
as well as the Tam thing. To be honest, the gun didn't seem
like a big deal in the morning anyway. I mean, it was
better not to have the fucken thing lying there in me flat,
especially since I'd started waving it about at the IRA and
all. Worse than that, I could end up shooting me cock off
the way things were going, fuck's sake.

So I picked it up and wrapped it in an oul tea towel I'd
had lying about the place. Some oul rag I'd never washed.
So I just did the oul movie thing and gave the gun a good
rubbing all over to get rid of the prints and all. I've no
idea if that works, but I didn't know any other way. I'd
never handled a gun before. Then I sort of tied the thing
up in that tea towel, so it looked like nothing. I put it in
me jacket pocket and fucked off to work. Karim would
get his precious gun that day, the mad Arab bastard. I'd no
use for the thing.

It was bad shit outside, so it was. People were out
sweeping up all over the place, giving off buckets about
the rioters and the Peelers and everyone else. All the cunts
who were out causing the hassle would have been lying in
their beds asleep, so they would. Peelers and all. For some
reason I got a bunch of dirty looks off these oul folks.
They must have thought because I was a bit younger and
lived up the street, then I must have been one of them
who was rioting. You know when you get a dirty look
from someone who's old? It looks like they're disappointed

in you, that you fucked something up or whatever. Well, I was getting a whole load of those. But I thought they can go and fuck themselves.

I gave a few wee sneers when I walked past, but I didn't mean any harm. Half of them went back inside anyway and you could hear the double locks and chains and all. Moaning fuckers. I mean, this was their mess in the first place, when you think about it. They're the fuckers who kept the whole thing going. Old people's memories are all cute and precious and all, but they're fucked-up memories too. They're never able to remember the shite they caused, even though it's staring them in the face. That oul Alzheimers is dead handy in a place like this, so it is. You don't die guilty.

So anyway, I just kicked me way through the rubble as I went along. There was a lot of damage. Loads of people have them oul brown grilles on their windows because the stones have wings round here. Even some of those were damaged. I mean, what kind of eejit fucks bricks at steel windows?

I remember one time when I was a wee lad seeing these boys running up and smashing the fuck out of the traffic lights near where I lived, a mile or so away. Some Taigs had been killed up the street by the Army and these fellas were going crazy. I thought they'd been going to brick my window first, but they didn't. Made a change, so it did. I just watched them run on past and belt the shite out of the lights with a big stick, and the things just cut out. They were laughing, and it was exciting and all, but I used to wonder why they did that. It was pointless, like. Fucked up the traffic for ages. It kind of annoyed me. The day after that riot, I felt like doing the same thing all along the street, right up to the shops. I don't know why, but I'd have been too late for it anyway. Every fucken traffic light was already smashed to bits. They're always the first thing to go. That's why they put those covers round them in parts of Belfast, so it is. You can hardly see what colour they are sometimes round there. I remember thinking I couldn't give two fucks about traffic lights anymore. I couldn't even give one fuck. It made me laugh really.

Karim was like a wee puppy in work that day, so he was. He gave me this big smile when he seen me walk in. He looks like a fucken eejit when he does that. He's one giant yellow front tooth and then another one further along. I'd say he's two missing, wherever they went to. I just played it all dead cool and all, and nodded and poured me coffee. Two of the lads were talking about the Ireland game and about some new player on the team or some bollocks like that. Cunts weren't even speaking to me at all. Just as well really, because I'd fuck all plans to talk to them.

Steven from Shropshite had put a notice up on the board. He'd taken down a picture of some girl fiddling with herself in a bath and put up this thing. It said Memo at the top. It was saying the Secretary of State had been very pleased with all the work we'd done for the Prime Minister's visit and appreciated that it was all done with very short notice. It was saying that we couldn't be told in advance because the Prime Minister had been over for urgent talks with the politicians and that the security was tight and all that oul shite.

Hugh said the Prime Minister had met up with a few party leaders and they'd all gone off somewhere for secret talks and stuff, so they'd needed loads of cars. The security people then wanted loads of different cars so that no one would know who was in what car if someone tried to hit a motor. That was Hugh's thoughts anyway. Fact is that most people were more interested in the fucken football than trying to take out the Prime Minister. That's how fucked up Northern Ireland terrorism is.

So Karim followed me after I walked out of the kitchen. He was smiley, but all cool and cautious. He just sort of shadowed me, just stuck to me as I walked about. I went over to the ramp, the thing no cunt can drive up but me. I still had that tea towel in my pocket.

He goes: 'Hey, you help me today?'

So I'm: 'Aye, I got it, you fucken loony.'

'Cool, man.' He was always saying that.

So I says: 'Aye, it's here.'

He goes: 'Cool, man.' Everything was cool.

So I opened the door of this big fuck off Vauxhall and put the gun on the passenger seat. I felt a wee bit nervous for some reason, but it wasn't like there was any cameras there watching us. I don't think so, anyway. I mean, you tell me. So anyway, Karim leans in and opens the rag, slips the weapon out and puts it inside his wee boiler suit. Dead cool, like.

He goes: 'Is fucking loaded, man.' He was shocked as fuck.

I'm like: 'Aye. Heavy, isn't it.'

Then he goes: 'Is no safety catch, Fletcher man. You fucking crazy cunt.'

He laughed then and I did a wee bit too. Fucken thing had been ready to go off anytime. Then what happened was I asked him did he get his hole the night before and he laughed again. I thought he'd come clean about it, but he just laughed and grinned like a dirty oul fecker. He fucken did, the bastard. I know rightly. Some oul street whore somewhere. The two of us started laughing like madmen and some of the other ones looked over like we were dickheads and we laughed at them too. The wankers. Then he goes all serious.

He says: 'Hey. We don't talk this again, man.'

So I says: 'No. No problem. It's forgotten.'

'Cool. We forget now.'

'Aye.'

Then he says: 'I fucking help you today, man. Any problem with this shit work, ask me. I fucking help you today.'

I goes: 'Thanks, Karim. But it's not fucken rocket science.'

He goes: 'No, man. But you know I mean good.'

So I says: 'Yes I do, mate. Thanks.'

'Cool, man. It's cool.'

Truth is, I had something on me mind that I'd have loved to say to Karim. I knew for a fact I could trust him and that he'd be a great guy for a bit of support and all. It was the whole Tam thing, you know. I was going to do it, like. I was going to strike the fucker. But I'd like to have let it all out of me head a wee bit and just told him about Wee Blondie's call and stuff. He'd probably have even done it for me if I just asked him. But that's the first thing the IRA teach their players, isn't it? Say fuck all. Need to know only. And Karim didn't need to know. I just had to keep it all inside me, to be as sure as I could. I was going to fucken topple someone and I wasn't going to get caught. Maybe it was good to have all that heavy stuff bouncing round in me head. I don't know.

Then later, about lunchtime, Steven asked me and L to go into the city and pick up a couple of motors. They were part of the thirty-one from the day before. I didn't care. Karim asked if he could go, but I was happy enough to get an hour away from the pit with that hangover on me. I needed to get me mind straight anyway.

We didn't talk much, me and your man L. Not just then, I mean ever. Liam's his real name, as you know. He's a bit of a lad with the other guys, but I never really got into their game. They spend the whole fucken time slagging each other off because of their religions and their football teams and shit. They were always bantering about politics and stuff, as if it was the source of all humour. But they were deadly serious underneath it. When L said stuff to Ronnie like 'ah sure what do you know, it's not your country anyway', he wasn't joking. They'd all be laughing, but you'd know the fucker meant it, even though Ronnie would think the same thing about L and his country.

L's pretty hardline. So's Ronnie. People like that are always trying to suss me out, you know. The weirdest thing to them is a person they can't put into a wee box. You could tell by the questions that they were always trying to work out if I was a Taig or a Prod. Green or orange, you know? Me name's Fee, and it sounds a bit Catholic, but there's Prod Fees too. And Fletcher means fuck all to anyone, except me Ma and Da. L had asked me about everything, from what school I was at, to me Ma's maiden name, to me girlfriend's name, to what street I lived on, to spell something with the letter H in it, to see if I'd ever been to a football ground and the whole fucken shebang. I never answered him. The way I see it there's no wee box for me. I don't want one. So I'm fucked if I'm going to let some cunt try and put me in one. So anyway, he started again in the car on the way down.

Here's him: 'Here Fletch, you see the match last night?'

I'm just: 'No.'

'We were hammered, eh. Fucken shite, like.'

I didn't say fuck all.

Then he goes: 'You live up near the Ardoyne Peaceline, don't you?'

'Aye.'

'Some shite up there last night, eh.'

'Was there?'

'Aye. Few Peelers hospitalised. Riot, like.'

'Right.'

'You didn't see it? The Peelers had been round hassling people again. Scum, so they are.'

'Nah. Missed that.'

Then he gets all expert and says: 'Me mate lives up there and says the cops were round harassing Catholics. They never bother the Prods up there, he reckons. Is that true, you think?'

'Couldn't tell you.'

Then he goes: 'Aye well. Some wee Catholic lad and his girl got done over pretty bad by loyalists up there. The wee lad was blinded, so he was. Some fucker put glue in his eye. Cops up asking questions, pushing people around. That sparked it all off, like.'

I thought then that it made sense that republicans reckoned it was loyalists. Loyalists have done that sort of thing before, so they have. But I was for winding L up, so I was.

I says: 'What sparked it off was the football match. Bad losers, Republic fans.'

That made him mad straight away, so it did. He goes: 'Bollocks. Republic fans aren't bad losers.'

I'm like: 'They are. They're fucken wankers too. And cunts as well.'

I laughed then, so I did. I laughed like fuck. L didn't say anything. I'd put him in his box. He was ripping. He was squeezing his hands together and all. So sensitive, like. He didn't know how to handle me. It hurt his wee brain to try and work it out. He was so easy to work out, so he was.

I make people nervous as fuck. Because I'm not republican, republicans think I'm on the other side. And loyalists think the same thing. I live in no man's land, so I do. People would just love me to pick a side and be done with it. Any side at all, just so I could be counted. But fuck them. I won't pick a nationality or a fucken God or a hero or anything like that. Why the fuck should I? I don't want any of that shite. I'm just from Belfast. That's all. That's enough, for fuck's sake.

We'd to pick up these motors at this city centre car park, but the lanky bastard who was supposed to be organising it had fucked up. One of his cars was still up in Hillsborough and we'd have to wait for it. I got into the driver's seat of this big black Merc. It definitely had to go back to Stormont. That's what Steven had said. It's a sweet motor, so it is. Maybe the best of the bunch, if you don't mind me saying so. Black upholstery, real nice smell, blacked-out windows, armour-plated, buckets of comfort. You could fall asleep in it, dead easy. It was still spotless inside and out, I'm glad to say. Some top Man From England had been in it, I reckoned then. Maybe the Prime Minister.

L took the hump and walked round and round the car smoking like fuck, wondering if he should take me on or not. Lanky, the man who couldn't organise the cars, told him to put it out if he was going to be getting into one of the motors, but L finished it first and then stubbed it out on the wall. He looked at me as he bashed it and all these sparks darted all round the place. He was playing the tough guy. But I can't tell you how unfazed I was by L. Me confidence was sky high that day and he could tell he'd be wise not to cross me. Hangovers make you short tempered, so they do. That can mean you're tough as fuck, so it can.

So this is how it happened anyway, how we met. You see, L ended up getting into the car and sitting there, playing with the glove box and all as I stared out the window. He asked me to switch the ignition on so he could play with the radio. So I waited for a wee minute, as if I hadn't heard him, and then I switched it on. He flicked through the channels. Then he started talking again.

He's all: 'Nice car this, eh?'

I just says: 'Aye, and clean. Thank fuck.'

He goes: 'Hardest ones to nick. Me mate knows a wee lad who nicks cars and he reckons the Merc Seven Series are the hardest to nick.'

So I turns round and says: 'There is no Merc Seven Series, you gonk.'

'Aye there is.'

I'm like: 'That's a BM. Seven Series is BM.'

'Ack fuck, whatever.'

'Aye.'

So he goes: 'But there's these ones, right, when you lock them up the whole stereo gets swallowed back into the engine so it can't be nicked.'

'Right.'

Then here's what I mean. The bollocks started trying to pull at the stereo to see if he could show me that it could be swallowed up into the engine, for fuck's sake. He could've just asked me to lock the car up and we could watch the thing, but he didn't. He doesn't think. He never thinks, so he doesn't. Anyway, that didn't annoy me. It just made me smile a bit. Then the front of the thing just came away in his hand. The plastic bit, the cover of the stereo, just snapped clean off.

He goes: 'Fuck it.'

I'm like: 'You've fucked it now, big lad.'

And he says: 'Bastard.' I think he meant me.

So then I noticed a wee thing you wouldn't expect to see stuck behind the plastic front of the stereo on a Merc. You understand where I'm coming from? Just this wee square silver thing with lines on it, glued on. The stereo was a decent Sony, but this wee thing wasn't anything like you'd see on a Sony. You know what I mean? So L was trying to work out how the plastic thing would fit back on, and I leans over a wee bit and picked at this wee thing. Then it just came away in me hand. There was a wee patch of glue behind it and a tiny wee wire connected to it. The wire went into the back of the stereo, through a wee hole. You could see where the hole had been drilled because there was still wee tiny bits of aluminium there.

To be honest I reckoned it was a wee tiny microphone straight away. I thought it would be just like the fucken Northern Ireland Office and the intelligence ones all right, bugging the cars. I thought then that maybe you reckoned oul Karim was about to wipe out Stormont or some shite. Or maybe you were listening in to the civil servants and the Prime Minister. I wondered then was the mike turned on, and I'm still fucken wondering today. Anyway. What odds.

But poor oul L couldn't handle what he'd done. The prick didn't even notice the mike, so don't worry because I never said a word about it. I told him it'd be fine if we just got a bit of glue. I said I'd put it together again when we got back. Wee buns. Then L started asking if I was heading out tonight and I told him I was. I said I was heading out to kick the fuck out of someone. I just wanted to say it to see what his reaction was, but he just threw the plastic thing up onto the dashboard and looked away as if I'd really pissed him off. I mean, for the first time, I was only being truthful with the fucker. If you were listening then, you'll have all that written down or whatever. Mind you, you'd have had no reason to record the likes of me then. I'm a much better target now, eh?

So I bought another bottle of that whiskey on the way home after work. I don't mind telling you that I was starting to get a wee bit nervous. I was up for the thing with Tam all right, but I just needed a wee nip of the hard stuff to put a bit of poke into me engine. So I tried to keep me mind off it and all as I walked on back. There was a cop Land Rover near me pad. Standard procedure when there's been a riot and all. Cops were just sitting there in the van smoking like fuck, probably wishing they'd done better in school. It didn't bother me one wee bit.

So it was about half six or so when I walked in the door. I didn't want to do anything but get this fucken show on the road. I looked out across the street but there were no signs of life at all from Wee Blondie's. I hoped to fuck she hadn't changed her mind and gone and told your man what she'd asked me to do. He'd be on the lookout for me then, with his heavies and all. But sure, what could I do? Fuck it, I thought. Go on as planned.

I turned on the news and they'd all this film from the riot and all. They were going on about what sparked it and the attack that left wee Seanie blind and all. The two wee lovebirds had them all guessing. I laughed, so I did. It was making my day, that was. Someone had been saying it was a beating by the INLA because they were two wee thieving shites. And someone else was saying, like L had been saying, that it was a sectarian beating by loyalists. So the fucken republicans didn't know if they should be angry or not. Artie Callaghan was on from Sinn Féin saying republicans were denying it, so it must be loyalists. He starts gurning that Catholics are attacked every week and all and that everyone knew it was loyalists. Then that cunt Lionel Rosborough – he's another councillor round my way – came on to say loyalists had done nothing. He's with the DUP, like. Dead holy and all. He said it was the IRA just doing the usual and beating the shit out of their own. He said he'd heard they were gluing people's eyes these days. It was like each of them knew for a fact it was the other side. Nothing else made any sense. Ulster logic, so it is. I had to laugh.

So here anyway. I was going to tell you this. There was a girl I knew years ago, an American girl. Dead rich, so she was. She came to Belfast with her friend to take pictures of murals and all. They were Irish Americans. They reckoned they were all spiritual and in touch with the Emerald Isle and all that shite. I met the two of them on a bus one day. To be honest, I was just sitting there for hours, going round and round the place looking at all the sad bastards getting on and off and stuff. You know, oul fellas eyeing up the schoolgirls, the fat cunts who can hardly get up the step onto the bus, people listening to shite on headphones, women who look like they've been awake for years and all that. I love looking at all those bastards and seeing how fucked up they are.

In Belfast the passengers all change in the city centre. They'll all be mixed as fuck there, but then slowly when you go towards one area or other the bus will start to get more Prod or more Taig. By the time you get to the Woodstock or the Falls, your bus is basically orange or green. It's class to watch. You can tell the difference between them. You could stick me on a bus anywhere in Belfast and I'll tell you which way it's going. And half the people on the bus put their head back and slip into a wee dream. They get away from it there, and that day I thought I'd go and look at them. Sad fuckers.

So the two Yanks got on just to do the same thing and have a wee look at the everyday cunts from Belfast. Anyway, they were on the seat in front of me and I got chatting to them. I had them laughing and all when I was saying that everyone on the bus was a sad bastard and their ancestors missed the boat to America and all this. No one looked at me when I said it. They were all in their wee daydreams, so they were. The Yanks were in fits of giggles. Big white teeth on them, laughing away.

So we all went for a couple of drinks, got pissed, got chatting with other people and all that crack. Then I took this girl Shannon outside. She was dead tall and dead skinny, so she was. I took her to get something to eat and ended up fingering her in Kentucky Fried Chicken at Bradbury Place. It was hilarious. She was drunk like, and she didn't give a fuck. Probably thought it was romantic having a drunk Belfast man stick two fingers up her in a chippy or something. I could hardly even kiss her, she was that tall. Anyway I gave her me address for some reason and that was that.

Then a load of months later she sent me this fucken huge baseball bat. I'd told her that day I met her that there was no baseball in Belfast, but that all these bad cunts on both sides had all these bats anyway, and the only reason

they had them was to knock people's fucken pans in. So
for some reason she sent me one, a proper American one,
right the way from Chicago. It said Big Max on the side
of it. I reckon she thought it was a lucky charm or
something, that it might keep me safe. I don't know.
Maybe she thought I was good with me hands. So I had
the thing lying behind me door for years, ready to belt
some fucker who came to burn me out or something. I
always meant to write back to her, but I never did.
America's a million miles away anyway, so I never really
saw the fucken point.

So I reckoned this was the very machine to do the job
on Tam that night. I only had about an hour before I'd to
head to the Cregagh Bucket, so I got cracking. There was
empty bottles of fucken everything lying everywhere in
me flat. I emptied the bin out on some oul newspaper I'd
bought to read about some fucker I knew who got killed
a couple of years back. Then I got this wee claw hammer I
found on the street one day after a riot, and I held up
bottles by the neck, one by one. I smashed them all into
the bin so there was this big deadly sharp glass bottom on
it. I got the bat then and just with the end of it I kind of
mashed the glass up into smaller bits, like the way they
make wine in Italy and all. The noise was like a train
braking or some shit. It really made the ears shiver. Then I
got out that glue that belonged to wee blind Seanie. I
poured the two tubes all down the bat and turned it
round and round, tilting the bin so I got glass all over the
whole length of it. Loads of wee bits just stuck to it. I'm
telling you, it was an evil motherfucker in no time.

I left it leaning against a chair and sat down. I opened
the shitty whiskey and had a couple of chugs. I kept
getting up then to see if Wee Blondie was there, just to

get a look at her before I did it, but I didn't see her. I had
to just do this thing anyway, and I had to keep me mind
on the job. I even considered having that fucken bastard
wank to relax me, but I reckoned it'd be stupid. A big tug
like that just drains the fuck out of you, especially when
we're talking about a serious load of spunk. That's what
they say to boxers too, so it is. Keep it in you. So I
thought it was best to hang onto all of it, even though I
was starting to get this real dull sort of nagging in me ball
bag. The spunk had been busting to get out for days. I
reckoned I'd hang on tight, at least until I'd smashed Tam's
face in. I was thinking that there must have been chunks
of meat in me cum by then.

So I took a couple of buses and got to the Cregagh
Road. Big Tam and three other fellas arrived at the pub at
7.52pm. That's what me watch said anyway, so that might
not be gospel. But it was before eight anyway. They
parked this oul Renault Laguna out the front of the pub
and went on in. The car was fucken filthy, so it was. None
of them looked over at me. I was just sitting on a wall
watching. I didn't know where else I could be to look out
for them, so I just sat there, plain as day. The bat was in a
black bin liner, just dropped down behind me. I thought
I'll not waste any time here. I picked it up and went over
the road.

There's a wee alley beside the pub. I just dropped the
bag with the bat in it down there. There was some
rubbish blowing round anyway, so no one would have
noticed. There was some cars going up and down and
the odd bollocks out walking and stuff, but no one
would have seen me and thought anything. I mean, I
could have gone and got a balaclava and ran about
shouting and stuff and everyone would have ran off and

shite, but this way was easier. I mean, what the fuck is suspicious about a man walking along the street with a bag? Anyway, no fucker anywhere knew who I was round there. It's not strangers who people have to look out for in this place, it's the bastards they know. So I scratched me arse before I walked in, so I did. I don't remember if it was itchy, but I just felt like doing it, as some kind of symbol of disrespect or some shite. It's like the way I spit on the ground whenever I walk past a church.

So I pushed the door open and looked round. A couple of fuckers looked up at me. You know the half-dead oul men who sit in pubs all day and know everything? A couple of them. This was a bit of a loyalist pub, even though your man Tam did business on both sides. One of his gang was walking up to the bar. Tam and the other two were sitting down at a wee table. I just walked straight over to them. I didn't know what I was going to say until I got there. The only thing I could thing of was Wee Blondie.

So I goes: 'Here, you Tam?'

He says: 'Who are you?'

'Are you fucken Tam or not?'

He wags a finger and goes: 'Don't be fucken cheeky, son. What do you want?'

I says: 'Some girl out there, wee blonde sexy one. She's asking for you, son.'

He's like: 'Fuck's sake. That silly wee bitch.'

I just turned round then. I didn't look back. I thought hopefully the cunt would follow me on his lonesome because it was only wee Molly he was dealing with. And then I heard his chair slide back and him saying to someone to wait a minute. I walked out the door and round the corner, picked up the bat, stripped it from the bag and leaned tight against the wall. Me heart was going a dinger. Fear's exciting as fuck, you know.

The door swung open and closed then. He stepped onto the street and just stopped, so he did. He was just a few feet from me then. If the fucker wasn't going to stick his head round the corner into the alley, then I was up the creek. Then I heard him walk a wee bit closer and I swung the bat back. Fuck, was I ready. He appeared then. He just fucken stopped and stood there. He'd a big red angry face on him and a fag hanging out of his mouth. He looked like he'd about two brain cells. Dead confused, you know.

It happened dead fast. He flinched when he seen me moving, but he didn't really know what to do. He ducked, but that was nothing to me. I'd already swung back, so I just tilted the thing down and ploughed on. I caught him on the side of his head. A big fucken thud, like. He was dazed as fuck and reached out, and then he just dropped sort of onto his knees and fell over on his side. He lay there, dead fat and still. The glass on the bat had stuck straight into his skin. Then the blood started running out of him, out of all these wee holes. He sort of groaned, so he did. He closed his eyes and then the fag just fell out of his mouth and onto the street. I don't think anyone seen any of it, although it would have made for good fucken viewing. But it was too late to think about all that witness shite anyway.

I fucked the bat away behind me and grabbed the fat shite by the feet. Desert boots, they were. He was one heavy bastard, so he was. Near broke me back when I dragged him down into the alley. His eyes opened and then closed again and he groaned another wee bit. I didn't know if he was dying or not. There was loads of blood pouring out of him. There was still a tiny wee scar beside his eye where Wee Blondie had scratched him. She's fucken mad, like.

So I picked up the bat again and whacked it down onto his face. There was green and white glass stuck into him when I pulled it out. I think one of his eyes had burst or something. There was a wee puddle of blood in the socket. His nose had moved too. So I just did it again then. After three or four times, as hard as I could pound the fucker, I started to feel his face sinking down under the power of the thing. Those fucken bats are lethal, I swear to God. I whacked it again and again and his head just started being crushed. I just stared at his face and the bat just sort of went up and down. Mad as fuck, so it was. I was smiling away. Laughing, probably. The blood was spattering all over the fucken show, all over me clothes. But the best thing was the face, all shredded up and slapped down halfway back into his own fucken skull. The whole lot was just going flatter and flatter.

I hit him about ten times before I reckoned I'd better wise up. I knew the cunt was dead as fuck anyway. I promise you. He looked like his head had been run over by a train. I couldn't tell which bits were his brain or which bits were bone or whatever. It was mostly blood though. I looked round me again and then checked his pockets. There was a wallet and a mobile and a set of keys. I just took the phone. It was funny that I was starting to collect this cunt's phones.

So I wrapped the bin liner round the bat again and wiped at the blood on me face a wee bit with me sleeve. I couldn't get the shit off me but I didn't care. There was more every time I wiped, so there was. I kicked a few oul bags and chip wrappers over him and went out onto the street and just walked off. It was eight then, by my watch. Exactly the time Wee Blondie had said. The only thing was that she'd wanted the fucker in hospital, and no hospital in the world would be of any use to that fat bastard. Fuck's sake. I mean I'd gone a wee bit overboard like. I watch too much TV, so I do.

Anyway. I'm fucken starving. Going to get a bag of crisps. Machine job, not the shop, so I'll be back in a few minutes. Don't go away.

All right there? Hope you didn't miss me too much, eh?
Want a crisp? I've loads of them, so I have. You name the
flavour and I'll deliver. I tell you, I always wanted to just
bust into that fucken rip-off machine. I put me boot
through the glass there and raided it. A fucken joy, so it
was. No alarm or nothing. That thing owes me, I reckon.
It was time to collect. Okay, Cheese and Onion. Nice one.
Happy days. Fletcher goes feeding, eh?

So anyway, big lad. I was telling you about flathead.
Wham bam thank-you Tam, you know. Wham bam Tam.
You have to laugh, like. So I went home then. I walked up
over the Albert Bridge and into the city centre and
jumped on a bus. You should've seen the looks I was
getting too. Blood all over me, so there was. I didn't care.
In me mind I was just thinking that I worked in a place
where they kill cows and sheep, so why wouldn't I have
blood on me?

So I went on home and just got into bed and sort of
stared at the ceiling for a wee while. I knew I was
knackered and hungover and all, but the heart had been
pounding a bit and I didn't think I'd sleep. Anyway, I did.
I calmed down and all and drifted off a wee while later. I
remember I was thinking how the Peelers would be
plucking the wee bits of glass out of Tam's face and
checking them for fingerprints and all. I couldn't have
given a shite about that. I just slept like a fucken log

instead. I didn't even wash or nothing before I hit the sack.

I woke up with the fucker's dried blood still all over me and the bed and everywhere. Stinking bastard. I just threw some water on me and fucked off to work. Okay, I took a quick check out the window at Wee Blondie's house, but there was nothing doing. As usual.

So work was shite as shite can be. It was boring. I was telling you that Steven had said there was Saturday overtime going and that anyone who wanted it could have it. You know, because of the big run on the cars and all earlier in the week? So everyone took it, and he didn't give a fuck. It's the only way to make your wages look half decent sometimes. Anyway, the day just dragged along. You know the sort of thing.

Oul Karim was praying for most of it, singing wee songs to himself and reading his wee black Koran and basically annoying the tits off everyone. But there was nothing anyone could do. His rights were precious because of being a Muslim so he was allowed to do whatever the fuck he wanted as long as it was religious. I'd have done it too if I'd half an excuse. I'd believe in any God that had me boss's back against the wall. It's common sense, like.

I think maybe L or someone had been saying shit about me because the four commandos were even less friendly than their normal utter hatred of me makes them. People are usually in better spirits on a Saturday shift because it's that bit easier. No one works too hard. But on that day oul Ian didn't even nod back when I did me random morning sort of nod thing when I came into the kitchen. I put two fingers in the air and he just ignored me. Karim walked in and said Hi and got a glass of water. He told me

I'd blood on me face and just walked out. It made me panic for about a quarter of a fucken second, and then I just didn't give a shite.

I turned on the radio at ten to catch the local news, but there was nothing about Tam's head. That was weird, but I suppose he mustn't have been found overnight. He'd probably have been found by now all right, but the news can take a while to get through. Anyway, I didn't want to be standing there with blood on me face, waiting for a report about a man who had his head bashed in, so I went on out to the cars.

Normally I'd just start on the ones closest to me, but that day I walked up to the end of the garage just to get away from everyone. I wasn't in the mood for any bastard of any kind. Neither was Karim, being too busy with his God and all. I reckoned it was just the right day to keep the head down and say nothing.

So then at lunchtime I remembered about the black Merc here. I hadn't really thought about it, about fixing the mike. I went into the kitchen and got a tube of glue out of me coat and went over to the car. It was weird because it'd been locked, and no one normally locks any of the cars in the garage. I went back to the kitchen where they've the wee cupboard on the wall that the keys are in. I got them and went back out to the car. I opened it and seen the thing had been mended already, which was strange as fuck. It was put back on as good as new. I don't let me head go too deeply into these things, so I just accepted it. I put on the radio, tilted the seat back and dozed off. Comfy as fuck, like.

The next thing Steven was at the door, in his casuals. Jeans and a golfing sweater sort of thing. He looked a right dick. He kind of smiled at me and I opened the door.

He's like: 'Hi, Fletcher. How are you?'

I'm just: 'Why?'

He goes: 'Can I just check something here?'

So I got out of the car and he got in. Really he wanted to tell me to fuck off back to work, but he didn't even have the balls to do that. So I stood there and watched as he turned the ignition off.

'Sorry, mate,' he says. 'This one's out of commission.'

I'm all: 'I got to clean it.'

He says: 'It hasn't been cleaned?'

So I goes: 'No. It was used the other day. I was about to do it and just fell asleep, you know. Knackered, like.'

He goes: 'Okay well, clean it and lock it and then get the keys up to me, yeah. I don't want them left out, all right?'

'No sweat.'

Then he goes: 'You've got some blood on your face.'

I goes: 'I know.'

So he fucked off and I got back in. I just sort of sat there for a minute, wondering what his problem was. Then I went hunting around looking for stuff. We're always finding things in our job. One time Ronnie found these photographs under a seat of a man and woman going at it. She had this wee Zorro mask on and he basically was screwing the hole off her, his hand over his face. There was about eight pictures in the set, that's all. It was one of the MLA's or something. Probably a religious one. Fucken oddballs, so they are.

Karim found some false teeth one time and a fella we'd here on work experience from some school found someone's laptop one time and sold it to some reporter for two grand cash. He was a bad wee bastard that one. He was just right though. Totally vanished after that, so he did.

But there was nothing in the Merc. I'm telling you, it was like it had never been used. I bet the spooks had already combed through it after the Prime Minister or whoever had been in it. I reckoned they couldn't have him leaving his glasses behind or his door keys or pictures of him screwing his wife or whatever.

So I was wondering then if the wee microphone thing had been to bug him, if he'd been in that car. Or did he know about it and it was him bugging other people in the car or whatever? It's all dodgy dirty war stuff, and I haven't a fucken clue about all that. You'd know better than me.

I mean, I know you've bugged cars before. You tapped the fuck out of Sinn Féin and all because Gerry Adams's mates found some device in his car one day. You wouldn't know what's going on in this country. Some reckon there's thousands of taps going on every day, some say it's only a few dozen. Fucked if I know. I couldn't give a shite.

So I went and got me box and brought it over. That's the wee box of tricks you use to clean the cars. The others use these certain cloths to clean the windows, but I never do. I always just use oul newspaper. It's magic for cleaning the insides of car windows and there's loads of it in each sheet. I wiped down the dash surfaces with a cloth and then sprayed some of the shit on the windows. I've nothing to tell you about that. Nothing interesting, like.

Fuck knows what Wee Blondie thinks of me. I'm trying to do right by her in me own way, but fuck knows what she's thinking now. Any man who hits a woman deserves a good bop with a bat, eh? Like normally, you know, you'd just buy some girl a fucken drink or something but this one wants you to kick some fucker's head in. High maintenance, like. I don't know. I'll think about it tonight.

I'll see what happens. Well anyway, if you've any suggestions, mate, let me know.

So after they found Tam, the cops went to Wee Blondie's house. Two cars were parked outside when I got home. On the news they said they'd found a body, badly beaten, down an alleyway. Cops reckoned he was killed there and not dumped from anywhere else. That might be because of the blood and bits of brain, nose and head all over the fucken walls. They said he was a well-known loyalist and that early theories were it might be other loys who'd whacked him. The cops were saying most of his drugs and prostitution business had been with republicans these days but that he'd still been involved with the UDA. One loyalist had told the news there was no way they'd whacked him because he was a Quartermaster and held in high regard and all that. The Provies said they knew of him, but ruled out IRA involvement in his killing and all this. It was funny to me that they hadn't got a fucken clue. It was only Wee Blondie and me who knew the truth, and she didn't even know who I was. In one way, it was a perfect murder. I couldn't have got upset about it if I'd tried. It was a success. It went kind of wrong, but it was still a success. I mean, it definitely wasn't a failure.

Then it seemed weird to me again that I still didn't know who she was to him. I'd always reckoned he was just riding her, because she's so lovely. But it could be that she's his kid. I don't know. Just because a man comes home drunk and beats up some girl doesn't mean he's shagging her, like. Or it could be his daughter and he was shagging her all the same. Fuck knows. I didn't know if I'd just killed her Da or what. Know what I mean? I wanted to ring and ask her, but I wasn't going to do that at the time. The cops were probably delivering the news about his being tatty bread and asking questions and all. I hoped they weren't going to be too long. I was thinking that the longer they sat around, the more likely the bricks would start flying anyway.

But they were long, as it turns out. They were there nearly four hours from when I got in. I just sat there, nipping whiskey into me and watching them going in and out of the house. There was no sign of Molly at all. Then some forensics pricks in white boilers and masks turned up and started doing their thing inside too. I didn't know what the fuck they were at. All in all, they took away about ten boxes of stuff.

Fuck knows what'd been going on in that mad house. I just hoped Wee Blondie was all right. I really did. I went to bed as they were wrapping up. No one threw a brick at them all night. That was weird. It was all weird as fuck. I remember I just lay down and cupped me big nuts. I was starving and sort of empty, so I was. And tired again. Dead beat. I was just wasted, without having even drank that much. I think I felt a wee bit like a murderer and kind of wanted to sleep it off. I don't know. You can never not be one again, after you've done it. I was probably just letting myself get used to it. Fuck, I need some fresh air. See you in a bit.

Now don't go freaking or nothing, right. I know I'm dead
quiet and all. I'm just sitting here with me crisps. I'm
thinking all this shit through. How long have I been
sitting here anyway? Fuck knows. A couple of hours, easy.
There's a lot of stuff bouncing around me brain and I'm
no genius at organising thoughts and all. Don't sweat it. I
haven't stopped explaining. I've just got to think a wee bit
deeper, so I have. You need to have a plan when you're in
my fucken position.

So it wasn't until about lunchtime on the Monday that
I seen the news about Wee Blondie. The *Belfast Telegraph*
was lying on a chair and it was saying that Tam's 17-year-
old partner, who couldn't be named for some legal reason,
had been arrested and was being questioned in connection
with his murder. Fuck me, I thought. Wee Blondie was
getting the third degree over something I'd done. I tell
you, that made me mad as fuck. The thing said there
might be a twist in the case, as she used to see some
republican that Tam had been doing business with. They
didn't name him, but said he was known as The Count. A
big fucken bell rang in me head, know what I mean?

The thing that annoyed me was the cops hadn't a baldy
what was going on, but they were still saying it was a
loyalist and republican thing. That fucked me off, so it did.
Typical Northern Ireland bullshit. I mean is there no such
thing as a fucken Crime of Passion or what? That's what it

was. If you kill some bastard round here, everyone thinks it's a Troubles thing. If they're connected to some organisation or other, no one will believe it's anything else. Promise you. Fucken pain in the arse, so it is.

I had this oul wet sandwich, but I didn't eat it. I just threw the fucken thing in the bin and walked back to the cars. Then I thought I'd go over to the black Merc and hit it a kick. And I did too. I kicked the fucken thing a right boot on the door, and it hurt the bollocks out of me foot. This fucken thing is like a tank, so it is. L seen me, but turned round in case I said something to him. They'd been holding Wee Blondie all weekend, the bastards. I swear, I was ripping.

I went over to the stairs and up to the first floor, down the corridor and into the Co-ordinator's office. I was like a bull, so I was. Steven near jumped out of his seat with the shock. Scumbags like me weren't supposed to be up there. It's prejudice, so it is.

He goes: 'Jesus. Fletcher.'

I says: 'Here, I've to head.'

'Okay. You all right?'

'Aye. Some shite just. I'm away, okay?'

'Yeah yeah, fine. See you tomorrow.'

It would fucken need to have been fine. I swear I'd worked there three years and I'd never missed a day. I'm never sick, so I'm not. I'm hardly ever late and I'm a good worker too. Karim caught me as I was walking away.

He goes: 'Hey man, you okay?'

I'm like: 'Aye, I'm just fucked off, like.'

He looked all stern then and goes: 'Someone give you a fucking problem, man?'

I says: 'Nah. Just fucked off. See you tomorrow.'

He says: 'Goodbye, Fletcher. You're the man, okay?'

'Yeah.'

'Smoke something, eh?'

'Aye.'

Then he goes: 'Hey. Keep heart strong, man.'

He gave me a real look, so he did, like he really meant it. I remember thinking it was a weird thing for him to say, but it was decent of him to be like that when he seen I was fucked off. The rest of the bastards didn't even look over when I was going. I just sort of shouted 'cunts' when I went out of the garage. Mad as fuck. Karim smiled and waved and then clenched his fist and all. He was wired to the moon sometimes, I tell you. I never seen anyone on their knees so much as that man was those couple of days. Strong fucken faith, I'm telling you. Deep, deep faith.

So when I got out and started walking down the Stormont Mile, I felt like coming clean. I felt like just ringing the cops there and then. It was like being kicked in the nuts to think Molly was being questioned. They'd think it was all some link to the IRA because she used to hang out with some Provie. The fucken PSNI can hold you for a week or something before anyone can even ask any questions about it. They'd be firing a load of names at her, talking about who wanted to whack who, about what deals were going down and all that shite. And all she wanted to do was get a coward back who was beating her up. But everyone was going on like it was a big political drama. Fuck's sake. Biggest shitehole in the world, this place. Biggest wankers ever, the Peelers in Northern Ireland. See, when you've killed someone? You feel like killing a load more sometimes. It becomes one of the options, you know?

So anyway, I walked the whole way into the city centre looking rotten as ever. I wanted a pub because I couldn't

think of what else to do. What else is there to do? I went
into that joint I was in before, the one on May Street
where me and the Arab were that day. There were some
wee booths to one side and I got a pint of Guinness and
sat in there. Then I got up and got a shot of some whiskey
called Paddy and took that into the booth too. I just
hoped no cunt would bother me because I was in no
mood for anything. Maybe if I hadn't killed the fucker,
just hospitalised him, it wouldn't have been like that. That
wee girl's life had just been fucked even more than it
already was. I put that wee whiskey into the pint glass and
then drank the pint as fast as I could. It made it a bit
tangy, like shitty oul wine or something. Then I ordered
the same thing and did it again, standing at the bar.

A couple of lads in this group were laughing when they
seen me do it. The barman didn't say a word, and neither
did the lads when I looked over. They were soon back
talking about how they'd spend their next dole money or
whatever. The wankers.

So I'm like: 'How much dole did you get this week?'

And your man goes: 'What?'

So I says: 'How much fucken dole did you get, you lazy
cunt.'

He's all annoyed. He goes: 'What did you fucken call
me?'

'Lazy cunt.' I was laughing, like. Then I goes: 'Are you
deaf, you fucken wanker?'

I downed the rest of the pint then. The barman asked
me to leave and I told him to fuck off. The doley told the
barman not to worry because I'd be going outside in a
minute. Here we go, I thought. I couldn't chicken out or
anything now. I just puffed the chest up and walked out
the door. It was stupid, like. Just one of those days.

So the four of them followed me. I got this slap on the back of the fucken head, like a really sharp jab. It was like I'd been hit with a set of keys or something. It made me a wee bit dizzy for a second. I hadn't even had the chance to turn round. Then, next thing, I was taking blows all over me face and head. They were all round me. Then I hit the ground and the kicks started coming. It didn't hurt. Not much. Kickings never do, not at the time. Every one of the fuckers got a boot at me face. I couldn't really see right anymore. I couldn't stand up, even though I wanted to. I think I wanted to. It was a fucked-up position to be in, I reckoned.

I was saying 'all right, all right' and all this, and after a bit they stopped. Your man came right down into me face.

He's like: 'Don't ever talk to me like that again, you weirdo, right?'

I just closed me eyes. I wasn't going to say anything to that bastard. Me day was already ruined, but I wasn't going to make it worse by giving that dickhead the joy of my attention. I said nothing. He kicked me in the face and the four of them walked off. I thought if I'd had a gun I'd have probably shot them all. One of those moods, so it was. I hoped to fuck then that Karim knew what he was doing with that pistol, the mad Islamic bastard.

A while later and I was on me feet again. It was just starting to snow, nice and heavy. They were like big white chunky flakes floating down to the street. I leaned against the wall of the pub and watched them, millions of them flying about everywhere. I don't know why they'd decided to arrive so late. I sat down and just stared at it all. People were walking past me thinking I was a refugee or something. No one threw any money or anything, like.

So after an hour or so I tried to make up the best of a snowball that I could and rubbed it all over me face. There was blood on it and all, but I was able to give myself a bit of a clean. That fucken snow was supposed to come about two months ago, but sure what does it know? Anyway, it was nice to see.

I kind of staggered about a bit after that. People were walking past me thinking I wanted to sleep in their garden and all. It was the brace of black eyes and all that damage to me face that was making me look like bad news. It was amazing that if I'd killed a bunch of people for politics and then put on a nice suit I'd be invited into half of these people's homes. One rule for the scumbag fucken politicians and another for me. But sure, who'd listen to me complain?

I'll be honest, right, and tell you it was actually good crack. I got a wee buzz off it all, so I did. Okay, me head and me teeth hurt like fuck and I was a bit pissed off with getting a bit of a kicking, but I felt relaxed about it all by then. There was nothing to be ashamed of by getting a hiding in Belfast anyway. Happens every day of the week. But there was still anger in me that Wee Blondie had been turned into some kind of terrorist by the cops. But it was only a matter of time before she was out, one way or the other. If they got as far as charging her with getting Tam fucked up, then I'd make sure it all fell apart. I didn't mind giving myself up, to be honest. Prison wouldn't be as bad as you think, especially if you were in long-term. You'd find your way, so you would. But don't get me wrong – I never really thought of that as a serious option. I would just have done it if the shite really hit the fan for Molly.

So then at the front of the City Hall there was a group of tourists listening to some woman rabbiting on. What the fuck she had to say for the place is beyond me. I mean, Belfast came up with the Titanic, the Troubles, the car bomb, kneecapping, Ulster fries and big fucken sinks. What the fuck is all that about? I mean, it's been great for churches and off-licences and journalists and all, but that's it. I'd be amazed if that woman could say anything positive about the place. I'll never know anyway because she was slabbering away in French or something, but I'd be knocked out if it was any good.

There was about thirty of them, all ready to follow a wee red flag she was holding up so they could see where she was going. I sort of joined in at the back and no one said fuck all. They just sort of held their bags a wee bit tighter, which didn't offend me at all. Who'd blame them? They just did that and walked on. I went along and pretended to the locals I was French. To be honest, I wished I could've spoken a wee bit of the lingo. Your woman might have been slagging Belfast off to hell. I'd have enjoyed that. Maybe there would've been something I could've learned, just about what things they find interesting. I don't really know fuck all about what people from other places think about. I never really learned nothing like that.

To be honest, I skived half me schooling. I was at it until I was sixteen, and it was a complete waste of time. The first secondary school was a big comprehensive up the Crumlin Road in north Belfast, and it was right in the worst days of all the shite. There were bomb scares all the time, and the school was blown up once. Then it was set on fire by a bunch of the pupils as well – half burned to the ground, so it was – and the Peelers were looking for a sectarian motive. The wankers. What more motive do you want than the place is a hole?

Anyway, that religious crank Lionel Rosborough went crackers about it. I was telling you about Lionel. He's a DUP councillor up my way. Anyway, he blamed the Catholics and the IRA and all for burning the school. He led this big protest at the gates to say Taigs were denying Protestants an education and all this. Half the pricks on the demo had torched the fucken place themselves, fuck's sake. A lot of Catholics got their heads kicked in over that. When the cops finally found out it was pupils who set the fire, Rosborough got the whole thing silenced somehow. He blames the Taigs to this day. I mean, what the fuck?

It was a Prod school, or what they call a State School. You know what that means? Well, it's just that anyone can go to it. Catholics only go to Catholic schools to be taught all that shite about virgins and sucking priests' cocks and all. So the Prods end up going to the ones that aren't Catholic, so then they basically become Prod schools. Me Ma and Da were a mixed couple, so I went there.

I suppose it was a bit of a holiday camp, but there were some real shite times. Like around the time of the Shankill bomb and Greysteel and all that. All that fucked a lot of people up in the head. Me especially, mainly because I got the fucken blame for it all, being half-caste. That's why they called me Sidewinder, so it was. Like I was some kind of sneaky fucken snake that slipped in from the side, you know. It's not like I could have done anything about anything, but sure that's life. Maybe that's why getting a bit of a hiding doesn't bother me too much. I've had a lot of those. The kicking and punching and all isn't so bad. They knew that, so they did. The loyalists there all knew that about me after a while, that me head was as hard as a concrete block.

One day this one lad came in then and got a bunch of
ones to kick the fuck out of me. They held me up against
a tree, so they did. It was after the school was burned and
all, after your man Lionel Rosborough started mouthing
off about Catholics being the enemy within and all this.
That set me right up, so it did. He might as well have put
up pictures of me.

Those fuckers pulled up me sleeve that day and held out
me arm. One of them was Rosborough's son. He had
brought in this thing that was like a cheese grater or
something. It was some kind of tool. I don't know. He held
that against me arm, so he did. He says this is what happens
to every Fenian sooner or later. Then he just ripped half
me flesh off, so he did. It all came out through this grater
tool thing like a bunch of wee worms. The amount of
blood was amazing. Then they just ran away laughing and
all. I stood there for ages, so I did, me head all fucken light.
I had to go then before I bled to death or something. I just
walked out of the school with this big red, bloody arm on
me and went down to the Mater Hospital. See when you
have to tell a nurse that you've been grated and you don't
know if it was a cheese grater or what? You sound fucken
stupid, so you do. I had to get stitches and all that time.
Loads of them. You want to see the state of me arm now,
so you do. It's fucken ridiculous, like.

Anyway, the whole thing drove me Ma and Da
bonkers. They were nuts anyway, but that sort of thing
really fucked them up. They were pissed most of the time
and he used to slap and kick her and punch her and all.
But the grater thing really made her lose the plot more
than anything else and she just kept on bawling her lamps
out after that, so she did. And me Da started drinking
more and all. Pain in the arse, so it was. I left. I just

vanished and hung round the city for a few days. I slept
rough and all. It was mad. I tell you, I know a few wee
nooks and crannies in this place, so I do. You see a city in
a different way when you need somewhere to hide. You're
always making wee notes to yourself about empty
buildings and all.

Anyway, me parents didn't even send the cops looking
for me or nothing. When I walked back in one day, me
Ma was sitting there blocked as fuck with a broken nose
and all. Me Da had left after beating the shite out of her
the night before and all. She'd sat up and downed near
two bottles of vodka. She was fucked. The neighbours
were all out on the street chatting about our family, so
they were. That was like the cue for the wee Prod lads in
the area to start doing our windows again. Petrol bombs
and everything came through every fucken night. We'd
moved before and all on this scheme for people who are
being targeted by paramilitaries and kids and all, but we
always got it in the neck wherever we were.

Me Ma was from Tullycarnet, from a fucked-up wee
loyalist family who thought Catholics were bastards. Me
Da was from the Short Strand, and his family thought
Protestants were scum. I don't know why they ever got
together. There was never any fucken romance or anything
that I saw. What was the point of going through all that?
Stupid cunts.

I was fifteen when me Da fucked off and then, just after
I turned sixteen, me Ma was away and all. I think me Da
went to England, but I don't know. When he was drunk
he always talked about going back to some girl he knew
in Newcastle who knew how to look after him or
something. Me Ma went to the States. She left the house
about fucken six in the morning one day, half naked and

drunk as a skunk, and was never seen again. Someone asked me had she topped herself or something and I said she probably had. I didn't know a fuck. But then I got a couple of letters from her saying she was in America. She said it was too far away and all and that we'd catch up one day. I don't know fuck all else, to be honest. She wrote to me from Boston, but I've no idea where she is now. I don't give a fuck either.

So I just ended up staying in the house and eating toast and watching Blue Peter until the Peelers came round and got me to this home for kids from fucked-up families. Your man Lionel Rosborough had sent them round, the prick. He got all the Social Services involved and all, saying I was the wrong religion to be living there and everything. He said I'd been starting trouble in school and had driven me parents mad and everything and that's why they'd fucked off. I told you about Lionel's son grating me that time. He was called Lionel too, fuck's sake. I reckon his Da put him up to it. I'm fucken certain of that.

See that place? Where the kids from fucked-up families go? It's really fucked up. I was about the least fucked-up person in there, I promise you. Then I was with a Catholic foster family in Twinbrook. I never got on with them, so I didn't. They were dead holy and all and tried to make me go to this new school and to Mass and cross myself and everything. I fucken hated all that. Fuck, they hated me there, in that Catholic school. The priests were all dead concerned that I had to catch up with me Catholic education and all, although they never asked me what I thought of the fucken issue. That's where I ended up getting another hiding or two, especially when the ceasefire came and everyone was supposed to be shouting up the IRA and all.

Then one day the mother, holy Bronagh, started thinking I'd the devil in me after that guy Artie Callaghan's wee Provie mates kicked the fuck out of me over the Monster Raving Loony thing and burned the living room up. She fucken turned against me big time, so she did. She thought I was pure poison, that I'd too much Prod and Brit in me and all, that I couldn't be a proper Taig.

I left after that. I was near seventeen anyway, so I just thought I'll go away to fuck. I'd got a job washing cars in this garage on the Crumlin Road, so I went sleeping in the cars for a while. Then I ended up getting the wee one-bed flat up by Ardoyne, near where I'd lived one time. It was all I could get. I worked in the Crumlin Road place until I got the job up at Stormont. No one fucken bothered me again, so they didn't. I've never seen a social worker since.

Load of shite, so it was, the whole fucken thing. But after all that I was all right, you know. I sort of got me head together and made things work. I just pushed me luck a bit and it all turned out okay. You've got to believe in oul Lady Luck, I reckon. You know, you have to give her a chance. At least let the oul slapper know you're out there anyway.

But here, the point is that I learned fuck all about fucken nothing. Listen to me, fuck's sake. I'm away off on one. I was telling you about that day in the city. That was mad, so it was.

Who the fuck's that? Hang on, mate. Some cunt's in the garage. It's not a showroom, fuck's sake. He's having a right wee nosey about, so he is. I'm away to talk to him.

D6–14. March 17. Wednesday.
17.50
Speaker(s): Woundlicker

Some English cunt looking for the Co-Ordinator, so it
was. No offence, like. He said Steven had told him he'd
be here, but I told him it was Saint Paddy's and that no
one was in except me. He's dead confused. He told me he
was over from Whitehall and all. I told him Steven was
away drinking with his mates up the Falls, so I did. Your
man's away, anyway. I hope he goes up the Falls saying
he's over from Whitehall, so I do. It wouldn't impress
anybody, like.

Anyway. Roast Chicken. Very nice. How the fuck can
you make a bit of spud taste like roast chicken? It's not
normal, so it's not. Lovely, anyway.

Right, so I joined in with the tourists. We went into
this pub called White's, the place where Protestants started
the United Irishmen or something. Some weird shite like
that. So I thought fuck this and gave the French tour the
boot. It wasn't up to much, to be honest. Not in French,
anyway. So I hit the bar before that woman with the red
flag ordered about thirty pints of Guinness and ruined
everyone's day.

Some French fella, a skinny oul fucker in a rain jacket,
was smiling at me, so he was. You know the way people
smile before they start talking shite to you? Just like that. I
didn't mind. He probably thought I was just fresh from a
riot or something, with the injuries and all. Me face was
all swollen to fuck.

He goes: 'Hello. Your city looks nice in the snow.'
Pardon the accent, like.

I goes: 'Aye. You're lucky. It's usually pissing rain.'

He goes: 'Yes. Is the Guinness good?'

'Aye. It's brilliant.' How would I fucken know, like? I'd
just walked in the door.

Then the barman asked for me order and I asked for
two pints and two whiskeys. I don't know why, but I
thought fuck it, and got the Frog a jar.

He goes: 'For me?' Dead shocked, like.

I'm like: 'Aye. It takes the head a wee minute to settle.'

And he says: 'Yes. Sometimes my head is not settled
too.'

I have to say I laughed. The two of us did. The barman
was a wee bit wary of me, because of the black eyes and
the bruises and stuff, but he wasn't that bothered. Thirty
Guinness-drinking Frogs were his big problem then, and I
was causing less hassle than that. So me and your man
stood about a bit while the pints were served up. I poured
the whiskey into mine as soon as he put them on the bar.
The Frog did the exact same thing and then says 'Very
Irish' to me. I felt like some kind of guide to Northern
Ireland or some shite. So I told him it was called
Fuckwine and we all drank it like that in this country.
Load of bollocks like, but he loved it. We clinked glasses.

'To the future,' I says to him. Fuck knows why.

'The future,' he says.

It's not bad, you know. Guinness with a whiskey in it.
It's not as bad as you'd think after you've had it a few
times.

Then he goes: 'So do you think the peace will ever
work? Will you people be able to run your own country
for good?'

I says: 'Maybe in a few years. But they're all up their own fucken holes now.'

He's like: 'Holes?'

I says: 'Aye. You might as well have a bunch of fucken autistics running the show. Dead smart, you know. But they don't give a fuck what goes on in anyone's head but their own.'

'Okay. But you think things will get better, no?'

I goes: 'Ack I don't know. Everyone's to blame but us. That's the way the bastards here think.'

Then he says: 'Okay. Maybe you take one side too?'

So I goes: 'Aye. The wrong one. I'm in the wrong fucken country, mate. I'd be a great Belfast man if I lived in your country or some shite, but not here.'

He says: 'Maybe you should. You been to France?'

I says: 'Have I fuck. I've been nowhere, so I haven't. Belfast. That's my life.'

Your man was dead on and all, but I have to say the oul mind was wandering as I was chatting to him. I was feeling pretty clued-in to what I was saying and all, but I was thinking about Wee Blondie sitting in some interview room getting shouted at by some ugly Peeler who hates her guts. She was probably being accused of being some fucken Provie or rival loyalist who'd set Tam up or some shite like that. They'd be asking her everything under the sun to try and get her to say she was part of some mad gang.

Then I'd a wild wee idea, right then when your man was talking to me. He was saying something about me cursing all the time, and I know I do, like. But it wasn't the cursing and all that I was thinking about. I was thinking to myself, fuck it. I just got a wee brainwave, you know. So I just said 'right' to your man and held up me hand and walked off. He probably thought I was a right cunt. But on a day like that there, I couldn't honestly give a shite.

The snow was still blattering down all over the place and I just went and got a taxi. I never get taxis. Well, I do the odd time when I'm pissed, but I hate taxi drivers. Most of them anyway. No one talks as much shite in this city as taxi drivers. Everyone fucken agrees on that, even them.

Anyway, I was in a hurry so I just pulled over this black hack and got in and told him to step on it. He just raised his eyebrows as if I was a right fuckwit, but I meant what I said. So I told him to step on it again and he sort of made an effort. You know, depress the pedal on the right, sort of thing. I said some cheeky shite like that. That always makes people do what you want when you go on like that. They hate your guts and all, but they do the thing anyway.

He turned up the radio and wasn't your man Lionel Rosborough on slabbering about Tam's murder and all. I thought to myself I just can't get away from these people. Some loyalists had been bricking the Peelers up the Shankill the night before and Lionel was saying it was a reaction to the IRA's sectarian killing of a loyalist and all this. Where do they get it from, eh?

He goes: 'Loyalists are not people who like to riot, but the lies and provocation from republicans has once again given them no alternative way to express their legitimate frustration.' He was going on about the Provies blinding that wee fucker Seanie and blaming it on the Prods, as if he knew it was a fact. Fucken unbelievable, so it was.

Anyway, the flat was stinking when I got in. I hadn't really noticed the smell before, but all that rubbish I'd fucked out of the bin was still lying there, just rotting away. In fact the place was a disgrace, to be honest. There was half an oul cooked chicken I'd carved up about a fortnight before sitting on the sideboard. And there was beer cans and broken whiskey bottles everywhere. I suppose I must be some sort of alcoholic. And that oul bat with the dried blood on it was still there, and the oul bin with the glass and the glue in it. Fucken rotten, so it was. I didn't know what the fuck I was going to do about it, but I thought to myself that at least I'd noticed it.

There was no life at all at Wee Blondie's house. It looked dead without her wee loudmouth charms, so it did.

So this is what I was at, right. I switched on the second mobile I took from Tam. The first one was as dead as he was, but the second one was still alive. The cops were probably listening in to it, but who cares. The thing started beeping away like mad with a load of text messages and ones saying there was voice mail and stuff. I flicked down through the texts and seen one from 'The Cunt'. It said: 'Ring me now.'

That was sent the night when I'd been flattening Tam's fucken head. Cunt would know that Tam was a goner now all right. I rang the bastard.

He goes: 'Who's this?'

So I says: 'Is this Cunt?'

He goes: 'The Count. It might be. Who's this?'

'Friend of Tam's here. We spoke before. We have to talk about shite.'

'About what shite?'

I goes: 'Fucken, I don't know. Money.'

'What money?'

'Wise up. Meet me.'

'Who are you?'

'Fletcher.'

'Fletcher who?'

'Fletcher the Fucker. Just ask about.'

'You a Peeler?'

'Am I fuck. Meet me alone.'

'Aye, right.'

'Why not?'

He gets all loud and says: 'I don't know who you are or what you want. Now fuck off.'

So then I says: 'You know wee Molly?'

He goes quiet. Then he goes: 'What?'

'Molly. Need to talk about her.'

'I don't know any Molly.'

'Wise up. You know her as well as Tam did. She's being held. There's some things we have to get straight, right? I'm a friend of Tam's. You already know that.'

He says: 'I don't know her, wee lad.'

I says: 'This is important. You have to believe me. You can't afford not to.'

He went all quiet again, so he did. Then he goes: 'I won't meet you alone. Where'll you be?'

I says: 'There's a wee alleyway round the corner from Shaftesbury Square, on Bradbury Place. As soon as you can.'

He says: 'How do you know this Molly person?'

I goes: 'I know Molly. She knows a lot of things.'

He says: 'What colour's her hair?'

I says: 'Bleach. Seventeen. No tits. Now fucken wise it.'

Then I just switched off the phone. I thought Shaftesbury Square would be pretty public. I'd just meet him at the entrance of that alleyway. He wouldn't try to pull a fast one on me there. I got me coat and put on a wee woolly cap me Ma gave me one time. Then I got the big carving knife from the kitchen. It was all greasy and germy and all from hacking that oul chicken up, so it was. I got the salt and just poured it all over it, on both sides. It stuck to it dead on, so it did. A whole load of it, for that added wee bit of a sting. I put the knife up me sleeve and walked out holding me arm like it was broke.

I got another taxi from the wee depot up the street. IRA cabs, it was called. It wasn't, but that was the nickname. All Provies making money. The jobs were held for them so they'd something when they got out of jail. On the same street people who never hurt anyone were on the dole their whole lives. Mind you, so were the taxi drivers.

So I told the driver to take me to Shaftesbury Square. Then I says the city looks great in the snow. He said it made a change from the rain and I laughed like fuck. He thought I was mental. He was probably right, to be honest.

I jumped out and gave the bastard his money, with a quid for a tip. I think that's the best tip I ever gave a Provie, apart from the time I told Artie Callaghan to fuck off and die one time I walked past him. That big sign in Shaftesbury Square was flashing away about the heavy snowfall. I just went to the entrance of the alley and stood by this big wheelie bin.

The streets were busy as fuck, so they were. It was home time and all the people of the day were running round, hoping to get back to their wee pads as soon as they could. All that nine to five stuff is a real pain, when you think about it.

This red Volvo pulled up, right on the double yellows, just where the traffic lights are. The passenger window went down and a man there nodded for me to get in the back. I mean, like fuck. I says no, and nodded for him to get out. There were three men in the car, all looking at me, dead mean. The man in the passenger seat looked round and said something to the fellas in the back and they nodded. He got out and looked about and walked over. I knew his face from somewhere. Skinny. Big nose. I'd definitely seen him on telly, at some rally or something. He was the one wee Molly used to be with, the paper had said. Tam's Provie link. He came right up to me, intimidating as fuck.

He's all: 'What's your name, wee lad?'

I'm like: 'Fletcher the Fucker. I'm not your wee lad.'

'What's my name?'

'Cunt.' I said it dead hard, so I did.

He goes: 'Whatever. Who's the girl?'

'Molly.'

'Who's the guy we're talking about?'

'Tam.'

'Okay. So you going to get in the car or what?'

'No.'

'Then hurry up. We're sitting on double yellows here.'

So here's me having the same feeling again, the one I did with Tam. Go for it. Hard as possible. I let the knife slip down into me hand, cool as fuck, and got a good grip of the handle. I'd only one shot. Fuck it, I thought. Just do the fucken thing.

Your man moved like lightning, but I'd me eye on him. I felt like a black belt at this shite. I drove the knife up under his chin. It was just at a tiny wee angle from straight. It went through his skin, up through his mouth and up into his head. Brain on a stick, like. It went right up to the handle. I heard something crack, but I don't think there's bone in that direction. I don't know. His hand flew up and lamped me on the side of the head. He'd no strength. I stood there pushing for a wee second, holding him up. He kind of stepped back and slumped down a wee bit. He was heavy as fuck. He was going to the ground then and I had to let him fall. I'd no chance of pulling the fucken thing out. He just stared at me the whole time.

The doors were already open on the car, so they were. I was going to have to run like a fucken fox. I didn't want to be taken away by those guys, know what I mean? I bolted over the road, between the cars, right across the traffic on the other lane and onto the Donegall Road. I flew down there and into Sandy Row. I didn't even look behind me, but I swear to fuck no one could have caught up. If you've just killed someone, you can run faster than any bastard. A few streets down Sandy Row and I turned left into this wee side road. I knew a wee back way there that would get me up onto the Donegall Road and then up a backstreet to the Lisburn Road. I thought I'd head for Queen's University then. There's always people round there. I didn't stop for a second. I didn't even slip, and the pavement was lethal with the snow. Thank fuck for those days hanging around the city centre. I knew the area well. Dead loyalist, like. Not many Provies know their way round there. I was gone like the fucken wind, I tell you. Before I knew it, I was sitting on a wall at the back of Queen's feeling like I was going to have a heart attack. It looks fucken lovely in the snow, that place.

So I took me hat off anyway. I just fucked it in some bush behind me. And then the coat too. It was only a cheap oul thing. Some oul tramp could have it if he wanted it. I was roasting. The snowflakes just evaporated into thin air when they landed on me hands.

Students were walking all over the place, carrying books and chatting away. There's ones from all over the world at Queen's these days. There always was really. They get well looked after and stuff. There's even more coming in to Belfast than ever. They've no idea about the truth behind the shite here, so they don't. That's a good thing, when you think about it.

Anyway, I sat there plain as day and no one looked at me. Me face was hurting. The swellings were really fucken sore when the adrenaline went away. I thought I must have looked like a right wanker, but I didn't really know. I was dying for a slash.

I dandered down Botanic Avenue. I was trying not to look as if I knew there'd been a murder at the bottom. I was whistling and all, although that's probably a dead giveaway. But I did anyway. I whistled the theme from *EastEnders* because it was the only fucken tune I could think of.

I could see the blue lights from where I was, from an ambulance. The Peelers would be all over the joint. But they'd reckon the killer would be a trained paramilitary or something. They'd reckon he'd be miles away, getting scrubbed up in a safe house. They'd know The Cunt as an IRA man straight away, and they'd be thinking it was a loyalist killing. It's been a while since the Huns used kitchen knives on Catholics, but not too long ago. I thought then that maybe I should have used gloves, but frankly, me dear, I didn't really give a fuck.

I kind of squinted me eyes together as I got to the bottom, to where they were stopping the traffic. I didn't want me big shiners to stand out too much. I mean, if someone said a man with two black eyes did it, and then a man with two black eyes turned up, they'd have to talk to him. So I pretended I was a foreign student from some place where they have black, narrow eyes and they're into *EastEnders*. Okay it's shite, but it's all I could come up with at the time. Me brain was away with it, like. Anyway, I wanted to see. No one looked twice at me. The red Volvo was long gone, so it was.

The wanker was lying there with a blanket over him. There was blood on the snow, really deep red. It was still snowing like fuck, so it was. The whole thing was a wee bit sort of arty. It made me think of when those Japanese wankers go out and kill seals for coats. They just cover the place with blood, so they do. Club their wee heads in, so they do.

So the Peelers started pushing people back and onto the street and all. There'd be traffic madness over it, being rush hour and all. I haven't driven outside work in ages, since I lost the licence, but I can tell you for sure that being stuck in a traffic jam when you want to get home is a pain in the arse. It doesn't matter if some fucker is lying dead on the street. When you're in a car, you slip into your own wee world and it doesn't matter two fucks.

I felt kind of hollow again, standing there looking at that mess. I didn't care about the bastard or anything like that, but something inside me was feeling low. It annoyed me a bit. I can tell you though, I wasn't going to let myself feel like that for long. I reckoned your man's run-in with the carving knife would be linked to Tam, and Wee Blondie was with the cops and would know fuck all about it. If the Peelers were thinking she was part of some paramilitary gang or some shite, then this would muddy the water and all. I thought it might work in her favour, you know. That was the plan, to do something to take the heat off her. I didn't know what would happen really. But I'd be watching out for Wee Blondie's release. Oul Cunt was her ex, so he was. A real charmer, I bet.

I cut across the street and dandered on down the Dublin Road. The Peelers were asking around for witnesses, so they were. I just walked on. I was on a mission to cheer up. It was something I had to do, because I'd done what I wanted and it had went well so I should be celebrating it.

I walked into some trendy wee bar down there. It was all students with hair gel trying to get as blocked as fuck. I ordered me usual Fuckwine and threw the whiskey in. I felt like lighting up a cigarette or something, but I don't smoke. But I felt like doing something extra.

So I goes: 'Here, give us another one of them whiskeys and a cigar.'

Your man goes: 'You got it. Pick a cigar, mate.'

He was from Australia or South Africa or something. He opened up this glass case and held it under me nose.

I says: 'That one.' It was the fattest cunt in the box.

He goes: 'No problem.'

He gave me that – it was eight fucken quid – and the whiskey and threw in a box of matches. He seemed like a decent oul spud, to be honest. I lit the fucker and took an oul draw. I looked around and hoped all these ones were having a good oul time of it in Belfast. I was feeling generous, so I was.

Anyway, fuck all that. I'd spent more cash than was wise and I'd nothing to show for it but that cigar and two black eyes. But I'm telling you, it felt excellent then. Just when I kicked off me wee celebration, I felt dead on. Life has its wee moments, you know. They come at you like fucken Frisbees sometimes and you just have to catch them.

It took me about half an hour to smoke that thing. It was really annoying people all over the place, but I puffed away at the bastard anyway. Hardly anyone will say anything to a man with two black eyes and a fat cigar. I drank like a fish in between the big deep draws, so I did. It was hard not to cough and I think smoking Karim's funny fags helped me cope. Karim once smoked this shite called AK47, you know, like the gun? I promise you, it's like someone holding your brain up and just blasting it with automatic gunfire for about ten minutes. That's probably why they call it that, like. AK47. Some days that stuff just fucks you out of it, but then sometimes you're just ready for it. If I'd had some then, I'd have got fucken slaughtered. Anyway, I got the Aussie or whatever to give me four more drinks – well, eight drinks – and I drank them all, no problem.

Then I remember I was wondering did the tip of that knife come out through the top of Cunt's head? When I sort of measured the knife with me hands, when I guessed at the length, I reckoned it would be longer than a man's head was deep. If that was right, then the thing must have gone right the way through. It would've left him looking like he'd a wee tiny steel shark fin on his skull. The stupid fucker. It had jammed when I hit the nub of the handle, but I don't know if that was because the handle had stopped at the outside of his jaw or if the blade had stopped at the inside of the top of his skull. Know what I mean? I'd heard a wee crack, but I didn't know what it was. I mean, a skull isn't that strong, you know. I measured the knife out again in me hands anyway, trying to remember what size it was. Two girls looked over at me and laughed a bit. It looked like I was sizing up a length of cock or something. I would probably have laughed if I hadn't been so drunk and swollen.

So a wee bit later I supped up and went outside. It was getting dark then and I was feeling a bit miserable again, fuck's sake. The Peelers had cleared Shaftesbury Square and were probably talking to all the loyalist touts of the day. Journalists would be going crackers too. A loy and a Provie killed inside a couple of days? Juicy stuff. Great fucken news week, you know. Long time since the boys went killing each other, eh?

I had to laugh. There would be all these sources talking about it in the papers the next day, so there would. No source would say it was a Crime of Passion. No one knew that but me and no one would even guess it. It wouldn't make sense. Not even Wee Blondie herself really knew it.

The snow had stopped by that time and was lying well on the ground, on the bits that people hadn't walked all over anyway. I walked on what bits of it I could, trying to hear it all scrunch under me feet. Fuck knows why. It was cold without a jacket or hat or anything, and going home to that fucken kip of mine was a right shite thought, so it was.

Then I seen this hooker up off Ormeau Avenue, on a street called Linenhall Street. You know, one of those streets with nothing on it at night-time, but there's loads of men driving round and round it anyway? That sort of street. I seen this tubby hooker anyway, a porky cheap brunette thing. Pretty enough, I suppose. Probably about my age or a bit younger. She was standing there in this wee skirt and white boots and a black puffa jacket. She looked pretty sexy to be honest, all cold with the chill creeping up her knickers. I reckoned her nipples would be like football studs, so I did. I was blocked, like. Then I thought fuck it, I'm going for it. Blowing me load up some hooker would've just about blown me mind, I reckoned. I love girls who dress like sluts, so I do. You can stick your long dresses up your hole, so you can. Fletcher the Lecher, eh?

I just says: 'Hello.'

She says: 'Hiya.'

I goes: 'Cold night.'

'Aye. You no coat?'

I goes: 'Nah. Forgot it.' I was slurring away.

She says: 'Right. What you looking for?'

'You got a place?'

'Aye. Up there in the flats.'

'Right. Come on. You've scored.'

'You got money?'

'Aye. How much is it?'

'What do you want?'

So I says: 'A ride.'

She's like: '£40.'

I'm like: 'Fuck me.'

So she says: 'How much you got?'

Then I goes: 'Is the flat warm?'

She goes: 'What?'

I says: 'Just if I'm paying, like. I'd want some heat, you know.'

She didn't like that: 'Here, go and fuck yourself, right. It's not a fucken hostel.'

'Aye well. Just a question.'

Then she goes: 'Fuck off.'

She was pissed off. I suppose I was a bit blocked and didn't approach it right, but she didn't have to be so fucken rude about it. She was probably giving a cut of her money to some player anyway. I looked at her for a moment and she just looked away in the other direction and started tapping her foot and chewing and all. When I thought about it, she looked dog rough, although I'd have fucked her all right. But she looked like shite. And here's me, I thought, pretty as a picture with me shiners probably glowing in the dark.

I just got a cab from there. Some cowboy with a home-made sign, chancing his arm at making a few quid in his oul Ford Escort. You could usually tell just by the accent. Real rural wankers, so they were. Farmers up from the country in the evenings to try and get a few quid out of dozy fuckheads like me. Half the time they didn't have a baldy where they were going in the city, but when you got home you could give them a couple of quid and tell them to fuck off and they would. All you have to do is tell them you're going to ring the Peelers and they soon vanish. They've no insurance or any of that shite. Tell them you're in the UVF or something. They soon fuck off back to farmer land, so they do. You have to use what you can.

I got him to bring me up alongside the Peaceline and drop me off. It's Provoland, like. But I was thinking that I just fancied a bit of a walk. It was quiet as fuck. The usual hoods were standing around, but they weren't laughing and groping that night. There was a dead serious mood. Something to do with one of their wankers getting a blade through his beak. A couple of cop wagons came down the street, but no one was bothered by them. A British Army Saracen was following, and no one even noticed. The blame for all this would've been given to the loys, and sure why not?

I think I was the only person having a wee laugh to myself, but you wouldn't have known it from me face. I put on this dead serious look, and sort of nodded over at the lads. They nodded back. It was like we all knew things were dead bad or something.

There's a gate further up, a wee small opening in the Peaceline. There was a big hoo-ha when that wee gate was opened a few months after the ceasefires in the nineties. Do you remember that? There were still a bunch of hidings going on, but because the guns were silent, the world reckoned Northern Ireland was all peace. The government loved that. So they got the gate opened and then said they'd been able to open the gate, and then the President came over from the States and everyone got really excited and shite. Every time things break down, there's always a few shots fired through that gate, so there is. But they always keep it open to show the world that there's peace. But that night the cops were just pulling up at it and three of them got out and went to close it. It took three of them, armed to the teeth, to do it. You could tell they were getting worried.

Anyway, I just dandered over. It was funny that it was being closed again. I laughed. The cops thought I was on the happy pills. I ducked through anyway. I'd be the last man to do that for a while.

I walked out into loyalist land, cocky as fuck. The first thing I seen was a couple more cop wagons. There was some lads there too, all looking a wee bit brighter than the Taigs. And why wouldn't they be? Some fucken Provie had just got a salty knife through his wee tiny mind. But still there was something dead bad in the air, so there was. You could feel it, like. The day after that the Prods were going to be burying big Tam, and they still hadn't even a fucken baldy who killed the fat fucker. I tell you, I was near laughing out loud.

I walked on up, as if I was local as fuck, hands in
pockets, scowl on the face, laughing away in me head.
One of the lads looked over, and I just gave him a wee
cool nod. He nodded back. If your balls are big enough,
you can go anywhere you want in this town, so you can.
Just let on that you know where you're going and no one
will fuck with you. Simple stuff. But it was a bit like a
ghost train or something in there.

It got dark along that way, by the Peaceline. I told you
how the hoods are always putting street lights out. I
walked towards home, towards Wee Blondie's house. I
looked up at me flat. It was as shite from the outside as it
was from inside, fuck's sake.

I turned at the main road and walked along. The cops
were on their way up, to close the big gate over. They
were watching me, so they were, looking at me wandering
from green to orange. They must have thought I was
mental. There was a big bright light on in the front room
of Wee Blondie's house. I walked closer. You could see
through the bars that the curtains were half open. And
there she was, the wee honey. She was sitting, tapping her
foot, smoking a cigarette, staring ahead of her. I don't
know if she was watching telly or just staring at the wall,
but she was dead still. And then she blew a few smoke
rings. I smiled a big cheesy one to myself and walked on.
You wouldn't blow smoke rings if things were fucked up, I
thought. You have to have your mind on blowing the
rings. She was maybe happy to be out. I hoped me dirty
work had helped her get out, and that she wasn't too sad
that Tam wouldn't be beating her up anymore. I know a
lot of women love men who beat them and all, but Wee
Blondie had made a decision to get revenge. I hoped she
wasn't sad that it had all gone to plan. Okay, I killed the

fucker, but the point was still made. He'd stopped hitting her, like.

So anyway, I went round the corner and into me building, up the stairs and into the flat. It smelled like fucken death in there. I said to myself that I'd sort it out the next day. But I felt so tired that I just wanted to lie down right away, not even have a drink. I lay down on the bed and, I promise you, I was asleep before I remember even hitting the manky oul pillow.

I'm just going to sit here for a minute now, right? I just don't want to speak for a wee while. I've too much to think about. This thing has gone haywire, you know. Fucken haywire.

D6–14. March 18. Thursday.
09.21
Speaker(s): Woundlicker

So, mucker, I told you. Didn't I tell you? They were
kicking the fuck out of each other yesterday afternoon,
after the Paddy's Day parade. A bunch of Taigs walked up
by the bottom of the Shankill with their flags out and all.
And then a bunch of Prod spides looking for Taigs with
flags got stuck into them. I hope everyone got their
fucken head kicked in.

Hugh and Ian are musing away about it all, so they
are. Hugh's blaming the Prods for attacking the Taigs but
Ian's saying the Prods were definitely provoked. Last
month a bunch of Taigs attacked Prods and Ian was
saying then that it was all the Taigs' fault and Hugh said
the Taigs were definitely provoked. Fucked up. Know
what I mean?

Hugh's priceless, like. He was going on there now about
someone busting into the crisp machine. He reckons it
must have been Prods who did it. He says Prods are always
angry on Saint Paddy's Day because of the Tricolours
flying everywhere. He reckons they were wandering
around the Stormont Estate and saw the garage was open
and the security guard half-asleep, slipped in, saw the
machine and smashed it up. So oul Ian's after coming back
saying that's bollocks because there were drunk Taigs out
celebrating everywhere yesterday. He says they've no
respect for government property so it was more likely they
wandered in, seen the machine and wrecked it.

They've stopped talking to each other now. That's what passes for chat round here some days. That's how fucken sad it gets. I'd be amazed if any of them thought that someone broke into the machine to get some crisps because it's a rip off. Fuck's sake. And you think I'm the mental one?

Anyway, the Peelers are coming up to take a look at it, to get fingerprints and all. I can't see them coming up this side of Christmas, to be honest. Hardly the crime of the century or anything. I'm just going to keep eating crisps all day and see if anyone notices. I'm on Salt and Vinegar now.

But fuck all that, right. Wee Blondie had got out. That said to me that things were better, but I don't mean things were starting to get sensible or anything. Like fuck they were. The whole place was just starting to go fucken crazy. It was just as well I'd had a great sleep, because you can't even start to deal with pure fucken insanity when you're knackered. I slept straight through, not even getting up for a piss, even though all the oul booze was sloshing around inside me like I was a washing machine.

The sun was bright as fuck in the morning. The snow was near all gone. I was feeling grand, to be honest. I was thinking about all the shite of the day before and there was nothing that really didn't fit. It all made sense, so it did. There was nothing wrong with it at all. I'm telling you, I was fine and dandy.

So I went on into work, said me Hellos to everyone, got a wee cup of coffee and started cleaning cars. No problems, no questions. Okay, there were a few funny looks, but I just said 'I kicked the fuck out of a bunch of wankers' when they were all wondering what happened me. I didn't look too bad and they didn't press the thing.

I reckon it made sense to them that an oddball like me would get the odd black eye or two every wee while. It was a few minutes before I noticed the Arab wasn't there.

I asked L: 'You seen that Arab fucker?'

He goes: 'No. No one has.'

I was all: 'He's probably away screwing a chicken or something.'

L says: 'Aye, Fletcher. Whatever you say.'

So I laughs. Then I goes: 'Hey, Liam, I hear some Provie got a knife through his gob.'

He goes: 'Fuck up now, Fee. Not today.' He was pissed off, like.

So he walked on, the sad bastard. I mean he didn't even know Cunt or nothing. It was funny. None of the lads were talking to each other that day at all. Their own wee cross-community gang had busted up over this whole stuff. They were all on edge, so they were. They still are. That's how good their friendships were in the first place.

The *Belfast* belly-laugh *Telegraph* came in at lunchtime. I took the fucker. Normally Ian reads the thing and then sits slabbering about who should do what and what a terror this and that are and giving us all the benefit of his ability to talk through his hole. But I wanted the thing today, so I just went and got it and sat down in me red chair. The murder of Cunt was all over it, so it was. It said a French tourist had caught some of the action on tape and there was a wee video snap of me running like fuck through the traffic. If I didn't know it was me, I wouldn't have known from that thing. Know what I mean? Blurred as fuck, so it was. So much for that shite. It said the Peelers were not ruling out the possibility that a rogue loyalist faction based nearby might be involved in the killing. And it said Cunt had been linked with big Tam in the past and that they were up to all sorts of stuff together.

The republicans were sure it was the loys, and the loys said they'd nothing to do with it. But they said The Cunt had it coming anyway. No one said he might just have been killed because he was a cunt, which he was. Clue was in the name, like. And then I seen at the end of the story about Wee Blondie, who can't be named for legal reasons, getting released without charge. I still didn't have any clue if that was because I'd done Cunt, but I hoped it was. It wouldn't matter if it wasn't anyway. He was no loss, like.

And then I seen the other thing. That's what really got me heart beating. Your man Salman Rushdie speaking at the Waterfront Hall that morning. Jesus fucken Christ. You know the big bollocks the Arabs all hate? Aye, sure you know all about this anyway. He was the one who had that big fat Fatwa – that's what they call it – put on him for writing a book saying Muslims were all cunts. Or he said Allah was a halfwit or some fucken thing. The paper didn't go into it. Holy fuck. I knew right away that's where Karim had got to. He'd have been busting to give Salman a kicking because he was dead fundamental at the end of the day. The thing said it was expected there might be a small Muslim protest at the hall for when Rushdie turned up. Fucken Karim would be one of them, I knew that for a fact. Weird-looking bastard, Rushdie. He'd stand out a mile anywhere. Then I remembered the gun. I wondered was Karim going to have a pop at Rushdie's ugly mug, if he was going to shoot him or what. I swear to God I laughed out loud. Fuck me pink. I remember thinking this would be mental as fuck. I just had to sit it out, so I did. Fatwas have nothing to do with me.

I went back to the cars then. I seen that our big black

Merc had been moved and that the keys weren't in it. I went into the wee kitchen cupboard and they weren't there either. I thought fuck it, and went up the stairs to the Co-ordinator's room. Steven was sitting there looking at pictures of cocks on the internet. He jumped like fuck when I opened the door.

He goes: 'You're supposed to knock, Fletcher.' He was pressing all these buttons and all, dead embarrassed.

I'm like: 'Aye. Give us the keys to the Merc.'

He goes: 'The Merc?'

'Yeah. The fucken big black Merc.'

'Okay, mate. Not a problem.'

And then he opened his drawer and took out a wee envelope and the keys were in there. He looked at me for a wee second when he handed them to me, and then he let them go. I don't know if he was a wee bit funny because I'd seen him looking up cocks on the internet or if he knew about the car being bugged and all that shite. I couldn't give a fuck anymore. The guy's a fucken spanner anyway. He stopped me there now, so he did, just as I was coming over to the car.

He goes: 'Here, Fletcher, do you know anything about the vending machine getting smashed up?'

I goes: 'No.' Then I says: 'It was probably political.'

He goes: 'Yes, maybe so.' And he's not even from here, so he's not. He has no excuse.

Anyway, Karim was nowhere to be found. I went on over to the car, opened up, sat down right here, plugged the keys in and stuck on Radio Ulster. They were slabbering about tensions at the Peacelines. Some priest was saying no one has the right to take life even if the victim's a terrorist. Boring cunt. I turned the radio down and tapped on the front of the stereo.

That was when I was all like here, get your ears on and started calling you a nosey cunt for the first time and all. Sorry about that, you know, but I just wanted to break the ice. I'd been thinking about the bug and all for a couple of days, and then I just kept getting back into the car. I couldn't help it. I started slabbering like fuck about wee Molly and Tam's house and all. And that was the real start of it. It all just kind of spilled out of me like a confession. I still don't really know why I'm at it because I wanted to keep it all to myself, but I said it all anyway. Maybe it didn't matter if the bug thing was still there, or if it was switched on or that. But talking makes me feel like I've told someone and that feels better than not saying anything. It's been nice to let the words get out of me head. Anyone listening would probably have thought I was just a mad bastard, and turned off.

And of course I'd fucken missed it. I got out of the car later and the wankers were all standing round the radio.

It was all: 'We are receiving reports of an attempt on the life of Salman Rushdie, the writer of the controversial *Satanic Verses*, at the Waterfront Hall in Belfast.' All that sort of thing.

No way, I thought to myself. But what I meant was, yes way, because I knew it already in my gut. I went up to Steven's room. He was sitting watching the TV. I just walked in and said I wanted to see the report.

He goes: 'Christ. In Belfast of all places.'

I says: 'Aye. So is he fucken dead or what?'

He goes: 'No. Some guy pulled a gun but they got him.'

So I says: 'What do you mean they got him?'

'They got the guy. They shot him.'

I'm like: 'Ack bollocks. Seriously?'

He goes: 'Yeah.' Then he looks at me.

I goes: 'Dead?'

He says: 'Yeah. Dead as a dodo.'

I'm like: 'Ack fuck, are you serious?'

Then he goes: 'Yeah. What's the big deal, Fletcher? You a Muslim or something?'

So I says: 'No. It's Karim.'

He's like: 'Karim? Our Karim?'

I just nodded: 'Aye. I bet you. Mad bastard.'

He's like: 'Fuck me. Why do you say it's Karim?'

I just goes: 'Because I know the way he thinks.'

Steven got all panicked and started ringing all these people to see what the crack was. I just knew it was Karim. No other fucker gives a shite about someone like Rushdie in Belfast because Rushdie couldn't give a shite about Prods or Taigs. I was right as well, except he hadn't pulled a gun. The truth came out later on. Karim was there at the back of about ten protestors – there were just a few cops on duty – and he had rushed forward, shouting his head off. Some plain clothes cop had spotted him acting like a madman and pulled his gun when he saw the Arab go for his pocket. Karim held up his wee black Koran and at the same time the Peeler fired a shot that got him in the neck. Then another fucken Peeler joined in and shot him in the head when he saw what was happening. Bastards. Oul Karim was left lying face up with the blood pumping out of him onto the street. He died just there, over the road from the courts. It was just round the corner from that pub we went boozing in that time. Fuck's sake. The whole thing was mad.

Ack well. That was that. Anyway, after I heard about Karim getting shot, I took the rest of that day off. I just said I was going and walked out the door. No one was doing anything anyway. They were all just standing around with their big mouths open and their wee brains confused. If you ask me, it was pretty fucken straightforward. The Peelers thought he was armed, that he was a terrorist and all. Al Qaeda or something. So they just shot him dead. Except they were wrong. There's nothing exactly new in any of that in this country, except that he was a Muslim.

To be honest, I was gutted. I was even shocked at how gutted I was, I was that gutted. I went and sat on a park bench for ages, like some sad oul man, and just thought about that mad Islamic bastard. No one gave a shite about him, so they didn't.

Karim was probably away to his heaven and I suppose that was great for him. That's what he believed, like. Maybe he was right. I don't know. He told me one time how some Muslims believe they get to shag a bunch of virgins when they live a certain way and all. So I didn't know if he was getting his oats or not. He'd have loved a bunch of virgins coming onto him in heaven, so he would. No fucken doubt about it. But he'd be gone from the Car Wash and, to be honest, that was shite. I knew I'd have to think it through, because I wasn't going to be able to just go on as if nothing had happened. I think me whole life was changing so fast that I'd to figure out what the fuck I was doing and what the fuck I was going to do about it. It's funny, but that Karim business made me think even more about things than before. It made me think more about the killing and shite. I was the only person in Belfast who felt like that just then. Just wee me again, for fuck's sake.

Then, later on, I just sat at home like a cunt. Me door buzzer went a couple of times and I knew it was the Peelers, so I did. A car and a van had pulled up below.

They were all hats off and all, so I knew for sure they weren't coming to do some raid on me over the murders. There would be a hundred of them arriving about five in the morning if they were doing that.

If I'd let them in, I knew they'd want to talk about the Arab. I didn't want to talk about him just then, or even talk about them murdering me mate. I just kept the door locked, didn't answer the phone or do anything. I didn't even feel like wanking now. And with nuts the size of melons, that's a big statement. The flat was minging, so it was. I remember looking at how dirty it all was and it made me feel shite.

I watched the news in the evening, so I did. I didn't want to, but I was interested a wee bit to hear what they said about Karim. Some human rights guy was on saying there would have to be a big investigation and all, but that was about it. They had his picture, the one from his security pass. Just a wee ugly snap of him grinning with his big front teeth missing and all. They said his body was going to be flown back to Algeria. They said he'd a wife and two kids there. That was news to me, like. I never even knew he was married.

Soon he'd be away, Rushdie would be away too and that would be it. There wasn't going to be any local trouble at the death of some Muslim. If he'd been a Catholic or Protestant, the rioters would have been out already. That made me think it was a really new killing. It would only be talked about, but there wouldn't be any more bother about it. Not in Belfast anyway. It was just an event on its own, you know. The way normal murders are.

The biggest story on the local news was The Cunt. People were on talking about republicans they knew who were going to shoot the whole fucken place up because of it. And then the loys came on denying everything again, blaming Tam's murder on the Provies and saying they knew people who were going to shoot the fucken place up as well. Then some Peeler was on talking about The Cunt's killer, saying they'd a photofit and stuff. They showed this computer mock-up of some fella. I couldn't recognise the fucker at all. They said they believed he might have been wearing earrings. Earrings? I don't know where they got that from, fuck's sake. I've no time for earrings.

To be honest, I couldn't take any more. I just lifted the telly up and dropped the whole fucken thing out the window. I didn't even unplug it first. Your man the Peeler was slabbering away about the ceasefires and all as the thing went falling down to the ground. Some wee kids on the street cheered like mad when it hit the pavement and exploded. I just closed the window and went to bed for the rest of the day.

That's all I did. I just lay there, half dozing with the green glow from that clock all over the room, and tried to get everything sorted out in me head again. I think it's all really come together now. I think I've got it sussed. I really do.

Look after me crisps, mate. I'll see you later.

Afternoon, balloon. It's me, Fletcher the Confessor, here to give you another piece of me mind. Or what's left of it anyway. I think the fucker's cleared off on me, to be honest. I've gone all empty-headed, so I have. I know what's going on like, but there's no big jumble of bullshit anymore. You know the way one day something burns a hole in your head? And then the next day your brain just chills out a wee bit? But the thing that was bothering you is still the same thing? That's me, so it is. That's me now. It's good. It's like there's a bit of free space up there. It's dead on.

Karim is dead, so he is. Dead as fuck. It still sounds weird when I say that, even though it's more than a week now since he got shot. I was saying it into me mirror last night at home. Karim is dead. I even looked weird when I said it, like I didn't believe it or something.

The day after all that, I didn't even go into work. Someone came and rapped the door. He shouted that he was from the Sunday something and wanted to talk about me mate. I said nothing, but it was like he knew I was there. He rapped away and didn't give up for about ten minutes. If I could've just opened the door and punched the cunt, I would've. But that would've fucked it all up altogether. So I just mooched about the place like the world was crushing me and shite.

To be honest, I was feeling a wee bit better, but I still felt like there was mourning or something to be done. So

I did it. I didn't pull me wire that time either, out of respect for the Arab. I think the lack of any kind of sex was making me lose the plot, so it was. It explains a lot about priests and all, so it does.

I stared out the window for ages that day too. I got a bit of a lift when I saw Wee Blondie come and go to the shops one time, but then I didn't see her after that. She looked pretty fucken miserable, so she did. I thought I wanted to ring her or shout out to her, but I knew I didn't really. I reckoned if I was ever going to meet her, I wanted to be in top form, not all bruised and smelly and miserable and mourning. And if I brought someone back to that flat that day, they'd probably have rung the fucken Army and had it cordoned off and blown up or something. Me with it too, probably. Disgrace, like. So I just sat there, watched her wee bum wiggle up the street and her wee handbag bounce up and down on her wee arm. I even smiled a wee bit, so I did, as she sort of stepped over what was left of me telly. She'd a wee red skirt on that showed all the way up to the bottom of her arse. I couldn't fucken handle it when she made that big step, fuck's sake. I went and sat down because I knew I'd start to drool or some shite, and that didn't seem right.

So I just turned me thoughts to sorting me life out. I just thought to meself that I'd make a plan. And I did. Sort of. One started to come together that day. I stared out at the rotten oul kip of a place in front of me, and began to use me busted wee brain. I swear, I stayed sober and me head just started weighing things up. You can't beat a clear head. The Arabs are better off when it comes to that. There's fuck all to be learned from getting blocked, so there isn't.

Anyway, that journalist came back again in the evening

and I let him in. He nearly fell over when he smelled the place. Don't get me wrong. I'd taken a wee notion and I'd bagged the oul chicken up, washed all the dishes, dropped the rubbish out the window and had a bath, but it still smelled like fuck.

I says to him: 'I know. It smells like fuck. I'm in mourning.'

He goes: 'Right. You okay?'

I says: 'Aye, I'm all right. Come on in.'

I could tell right away he was sneaky as fuck, this fella. His eyes were all over the show, into every nook and cranny in the place. I didn't give a fuck. I just let him do his thing.

I'm all: 'Wanna cup of tea.'

He's like: 'No thanks.' He'd smelled the kitchen. I don't think he wanted to drink from one of me cups.

He asked about the Arab, and I put him right. I says: 'I want a favour from you, big lad. Then I'll tell you all about the Arab.'

He goes: 'Okay. I'll want pictures of you.'

So I says: 'No bother. For Sunday's paper?'

He says: 'Aye. And I want to be sure you won't talk to any other reporters.'

I says: 'No bother.'

So he says: 'Okay. What do you want?'

I goes: 'One, I want a couple of grand in cash. That's a fair price for a good story. I'll tell you everything about the Arab for that. I've got a note he left me, I'll tell you all about the drugs me and him took up at Stormont and all that. And I'll just want you to help me out with a bit of information. On the quiet, like. I'll never mention your name.'

He says to me: 'What sort of information?'

I just says: 'Information a journalist would have. Any good journalist in Belfast.'

'Okay. I'll do what I can.'

I goes: 'Cash first. I promise you, this'll be the biggest fucken story of your life.'

Your man just nodded at me. I don't know if he believed me or not, but he should have. Maybe he'd worked on bigger stories, I don't know. But this interview, about Karim and all, would be big enough. People from all over the world were interested in it, so they were. Interested in the Muslims, anyway.

So he did his bit. He went away and came back with a photographer and the cash. We sat there for an hour talking about Karim. I was the only one who ever knew the fucker. I told him all this shite about him saying I was the only one who ever knew the fucker. I told him all this shite about him saying the West was fucked and all, but that he wasn't violent. I said he might have wanted to kill a dog that barked a lot, but that was it.

The photographer walked round and round me taking snaps, so he did. He kept taking them of me face and your man got on to asking me what happened with the black eyes. I told him me and Karim had been out and a bunch of Huns had started slagging him off for being Muslim and dark and all. I said we got stuck into them and kicked the fuck out of them. I said Karim hadn't a mark on him because he was shit hot at doing all the oul Ninja and karate and shit. That bit was bollocks, but you could see the reporter shuffling in his seat as if he'd shit himself with excitement. After all that, the guy gave me what I needed to know and we said our goodbyes.

Then I looked all over the place, but there were no cops anywhere to be seen. It was weird. I walked on out

and bought a fucken chicken fried rice at the takeaway
and came back in. I sat there eating the thing, wondering
how Wee Blondie would feel when I arrived at her door. I
just hoped she wasn't planning to move out or something.

I watched that house like a hawk for the rest of the day.
Me door knocked a bunch of times and the phone that
never rings rang so much that I pulled it out of the wall
and fucked it out the window too. But there wouldn't
have been more than a few minutes at any one time when
I wasn't watching for Wee Blondie. I seen her only that
one time when she went out to the shops. She just looked
like she'd the weight of a whole load of shite pressing
down on top of her. It makes the shoulders hunch up and
all. I've felt it myself. The rest of the time I just stared into
space. The oul baseball bat, Big Max, was leaning against
the wall by me table and I must have went and got it and
sat back down on a chair by the window. Anyway, I had it
in me hands for a long time. I was just picking off the wee
dried bits of Tam's face from the glass and flicking them
out onto the street. It would give the rats a snack anyway,
I reckoned.

It was probably Steven who would've been looking for
me mostly. I have to say that I hadn't even mentioned to
him I was taking the day off. I'd just explain it the next
day. It seemed like bad form because they'd always been
decent to me when it came to official sort of dealings. But
in the big scheme of things, as they say, my day off was
fuck all squared.

What else was I at? Oh aye, I did a bunch of press-ups.
I did about thirty in one go. And then I did another
twenty or so a few minutes after that. So I just worked
away at that there for a bit until me shoulders hurt. I
reckoned there wasn't really any other sort of exercise I

could do. So I sort of jumped up and down a lot and started swinging me wee claw hammer around and stuff like that, even though the whole fucken thing was pointless. But it made me think that it couldn't be too hard to get dead fit and all, if you put your mind to it. Fuck the shitty food, fuck the drink and all and just get active. If you want the end result, then just do what you have to do. Simple, really.

I didn't go out again. Later on I just bagged up the rest of the shite in me flat. After your man left, I took this wee notion to give it a proper cleaning, you know. I got the iron, the knives and forks, the bed clothes, the bastard clock and all that stuff and put it all into bin liners. I just kind of began stripping the place. I took the curtains down and put them in too. I stacked the furniture against the wall. I cleaned out the toilet and the bath. And when the cupboards and the rooms were all empty, I started washing the place down with soapy water. It was good as new in a few hours. Fucken gleaming like never before, so it was. And when I was done filling the black bin liners with everything, I just fucked them out the window with the rest of the crap. I threw a lot of shit out, so I did. It was like a rubbish dump on the street, but no one was bothered. And I kept me wee claw hammer. I wanted that. I kept me cheap oul blue interview suit too and put it on. I'd been a bit fatter when I first wore that, so it looked like fuck all, but it was good enough for me. I'd only had a pair of oul white trainers to wear with it, but that didn't matter a fuck. I put all that on with me one half decent white shirt and black tie and then sat by the window again. I thought that suit and the boiler suit would be me only clothes now.

I went back to work then on the Thursday and everyone was dead fucken unsympathetic. Steven basically

avoided me and not one of those fuckers has said sorry
about the death of me mate. I knew it was the right idea
to tell that journalist all me workmates were miserable
fuckers. Truth hurts, like. And basically I just spent the
next two days, and then this week, just sitting here on me
hole talking to you.

On Monday things got a wee bit exciting because the
story about Karim had run in the paper over the weekend,
on the front page and all. Steven went bananas. I've never
seen a man so ripping. He said the cops would be in to
question me about taking drugs on government property
and all that, and that I'd have to be disciplined and I'd
probably be suspended or fired. He shouted at me face for
about five fucken minutes, just from the moment I came in.
He said what annoyed him most was me saying that one of
me bosses liked to look up cocks on the internet and that
this had disgusted the Arab and all. He told me he'd a lot of
legitimate web surfing to do and that I didn't understand
his job and all.

I just said he'd got the wrong end of the stick. I said the
paper had just made the whole thing up and I'd already
spoken to me team of lawyers about suing and all this.

Nothing much else happened after that. Everyone just
huffed with me mostly, and that made no odds at all. As I
said, I've been doing fuck all this week. I haven't even
really eaten anything but bags of fucken crisps. I've just
been sitting here talking like a dickhead whenever I've
had the chance.

I know you're there, you know. I know you're listening.
I can feel it in me water. I think Steven knows something
too, so I do. He's just being a bit weird, a bit more weird
than usual. He's always taking the keys out of this car in
the evenings and putting them in his drawer. And then in

the mornings, just after I come in, he comes down and takes them out of that envelope and hangs them up in the cupboard. The car hasn't been booked out at all. I'm in it every day, and he hasn't said anything to me or asked for it to be moved or anything. He hasn't even looked in it lately. If he did, he'd see all the crisp bags and all, but nothing's been said. It's dead weird.

So the deal is you sit tight and I'll be back here in the morning, right? I know it's a Saturday and there's no overtime going this week and all that, but I'm coming in on me own anyway. Trust me. I've got it all sorted and I'll be here early to take care of a bit of business, like. I'll come in and keep you informed. Apart from that, I'm done with this shithole. Know what I mean? I'm finished cleaning other people's cars. I'm aiming a wee bit fucken higher. Life is now. Know what I mean? See you later, mate.

Morning, hero. Have a good night, did you? I don't know
if you're cooped up in some base in Belfast or sitting in
London or what, but I hope you got out and enjoyed
yourself anyway. You might as well, if you can. Friday
night and all that. Good time to relax.

So you want to hear what I did or what? You won't
believe it, mate. Took a walk on the wild side, so I did. Set
me grooves on the move, so I did. Happy fucken days,
like. Get that pen ready, big lad. You'll enjoy this.

Right? It was midnight before I went out. It would
have been earlier, but it was only then I was ready in the
oul head to cross over the road to Wee Blondie's. I was in
the suit – it's a bit dirty now, like – and I just slipped out
like a sneaky wee fox. Instead of what I would have
normally done, gone down the stairs or the lift and onto
the street, I went down to the ground floor and knocked
the door of this bloke I'd talked to once. I didn't even
want the likes of you cunts watching me going out,
although we both know at this stage that you're not
exactly putting me off me game or anything. But this was
just too personal at the time, even for you, big lad.

So anyway, your man opened the door. Big fat fucker
with an addiction to chips. He's called Stanley or Sam or
Bob or some fucken thing. One time I opened the front
door for him when he was carrying a shitload of
shopping. Frozen chips, mostly. We'd talked that day for

about two minutes about the place being a hole and chips and all that. I knew he'd remember me.

I goes: 'Hiya. I'm from upstairs.'

He's like: 'What about you?'

He was half asleep. A bit pissed or stoned or something by the looks of it too.

I'm like: 'Do us a favour. Let us go out your window would you?'

He goes: 'Aye, no problem.'

Oh aye, and then I says to him: 'Here, I'm sorry but I nicked a postcard from your letterbox one day. Some girl on a beach. Nude, like.'

He goes: 'Don't worry about it. I've loads of them.' He's dead on, like.

So anyway, that was it. I walked through his wee flat, hopped out and ducked across the road. There was nothing that made it look like I was being watched. I walked straight up and knocked Wee Blondie's door, confident as fuck. There was a bell, but when I pressed it there was no noise. Then I seen something move inside, through the glass.

She goes: 'Who's that?'

I says: 'Molly. It's Fletcher.'

'Fletcher?'

'Aye.'

She opens the door, cautious as fuck, looking at me and then looking up and down the street. Her eyes looked a wee bit glazed. She'd been on the vodka, so she had. Big thirst on her for vodka, so she has.

She's like: 'Fletcher?'

I goes: 'Aye. From the phone.'

She says: 'Right. Come in.'

She opened the door on up and checked me up and down in case I'd a big baseball bat or something.

The place ponged a bit, like me own dump. I asked her was she staying here, or would she be moving out or what.

She says: 'Fuck, I don't know.' She said it was Tam's house and no one except the Peelers had been round since he got his pan knocked in.

So she was wearing this wee white top, showing her midriff. That's probably the sexiest part of a woman that you don't have to cover up, you know. They have to be in good shape though. Pretty good shape, anyway. Wee Blondie has a wee tight stomach and wee petite hips. There was a couple of scars on her face, probably because she wasn't wearing any make-up. She'd be covering them up, I was thinking, whenever she goes to go out.

I says: 'So are you all right? I heard you were arrested.'

She goes: 'Aye, I'm okay. Who the fuck are you anyway?'

I says: 'I live over the road. I just wanted to help you, you know.'

She says: 'Come on in.'

So she closed the front door anyway and we walked into the living room. It was even worse than it was the time I sneaked in and nicked your man's phone. There were cans and rubbish and all sorts of oul shite lying round the place. So she took out a cigarette and offered me one. Her hand was shaking a bit when she lit it. There were marks all over her wrists, so there were. She blew out a bunch of smoke and then rubbed her head. Then she folded her arms and started flicking away at the ash on her fag. I was just kind of staring at her. I must have seemed a bit pervy or something.

She goes: 'Did you kill Tam then?'

So I says: 'Aye.'

She goes: 'Why?'

So I says: 'I just hit the fucker too hard, you know.'

She says: 'No. I mean why did you want to hit him so hard.'

'Because.'

'Because what?'

So I says: 'Because he was a cunt. I know he smacked you about and all. I seen you after you'd been hit one day, up by the shops.'

She says: 'You know he used to be a fucken UDA Quartermaster?'

I goes: 'Aye. Well I do now. But I don't care. He shouldn't have hit you.'

She looked away and then back at me. She blew out more smoke then and sort of laughed. I smiled, so I did. A big fucken grin. Cheesy bastard.

She goes: 'You're fucken bonkers. You know that?'

I goes: 'Aye. Crime of Passion, Molly. Fuck the politics. I just hated what he did to you.'

So she says: 'Crime of Passion?'

I goes: 'Aye.'

She says: 'A lot of people want to know who did his head in.'

I says: 'Who? Loyalists?'

She says: 'Everyone. Provies and all. It's a mystery, like.'

So I goes: 'Not to me, it's not.'

Then she's like: 'Sure then your man Cunt got killed and all.'

I says: 'I know.'

'You know I was with him too? Before Tam?'

'Aye. I thought you might have been.' Then I did the big cheesy grin again, fuck's sake.

So she's: 'Here, you didn't fucken kill him too, did you?'

I says: 'Aye. I thought it'd help you. Fuck things up a bit, muddy the water. I knew the Peelers were looking for someone to blame and all they had was you.'

She didn't say anything then for a wee bit. I suppose I was unloading a lot of shite I'd got used to having in me head, but that was still heavy as fuck to other people.

So wee Molly shook her wee blonde head and flicked away like fuck at her fag again then for a while. She flicked it about a million times, so she did. I don't know how it stayed together. The wee red end looked like it was going to fall off any second. I didn't say anything. Then she started chatting away again.

She goes: 'They think it's got something to do with me because I used to be with both of them.'

I says then: 'Do you like that kind of man?'

'I didn't have much of a choice.'

I says again: 'Do you like that kind of man?'

'No. I just don't have anything else. It's a long story. Sometimes you have to just take what you can get. Don't ask.'

I says: 'Okay. Fair enough.' Then I goes: 'I hate paramilitaries. I don't care what side they're on.'

She goes: 'Aye. I know what you mean.'

I says: 'You're very sexy, you know that. Very beautiful.'

Then she looked away and laughed again. Kind of nervous laugh, so it was.

She says: 'You know, no man has ever done fuck all for me before. And now, fucken hell, I don't know what to say.'

'Yeah. Mad as fuck. Sorry. If you want, you can tell the cops about me. It doesn't matter now.'

She goes: 'What the fuck do I want to help the cops for?'

'I don't know. I don't want you to think you have to protect me or anything.'

She says: 'I've told them nothing and I'm not going to start now.' Fucken star, so she is.

Then she goes: 'You kill anyone before all this?'

I just says: 'No. Never.'

To be honest, we didn't really talk that much. She went and got me a cup of tea and herself a big vodka and Coke. She told me a bit about some of the shite she'd seen, and you don't need to know that. Basically, she'd been forced into some shitty situations, you know. And she'd taken a lot of drugs and stuff. Then she told me about her time with the cops. They weren't too hard on her, she said. They insulted her a wee bit, to get her all riled up, but it didn't work. She was used to being insulted.

There were lots of silences. Sometimes she just looked at me and laughed, and then sometimes she just looked at me like I'd just turned purple or some shite. But there was a really good wee feeling going on between us, as if we knew most of the shite we'd put up with.

I don't really remember looking around much or saying much at all. I think I just stared at her a lot. I loved the way she spoke. Just like wee breaths. The wankers who'd used her in the past hadn't a fucken clue about the good things in life, I reckoned. She was their wee whore. But that only tells you about them. It doesn't say anything about her. After a while she asked me why I was called Fletcher. No one ever asked me that before.

I says: 'Me Da was a big fan of Ronnie Barker, so he was. And me Ma always liked some story about a man who did a famous mutiny on a ship or something. They didn't want to call me William or Seamus or anything like that. She was a Prod and he was a Taig, you know.'

She says: 'Aye. So what the fuck's Ronnie Barker got to do with anything?'

And I goes: 'He was called Fletcher in that show *Porridge*. You never see it? It's set in a prison. It's dead good.'

She didn't know if she had or not. She said she hated television and I grinned like fuck again. I looked at her legs then, remembering how she made that big wide step in the wee mini skirt over me oul telly. And then we didn't say anything again. She smoked another fag and just sort of stared out the window. Then she started to blow smoke rings again. I knew she didn't want me to leave. I just knew it.

Then after another wee while she said she was going to bed. She told me she didn't know what was going through her head, but she wanted me to come upstairs with her. She said I didn't have to. Fucken hell, like. Oul Fletcher was happy to go fetch, I have to say. So we went up the stairs, turning round at the top and walked into the room she must've shared with Tam. It was a right mess. Fag butts all over the place, a big cracked mirror on the wall and a dirty oul Ulster flag on the floor with booze and blood stains all over it. I looked out the window – there was a couple of bars on it, so there was – and up to me flat. It looked like fuck all.

Then she told me to sit on the bed. She stood in front of me and said she thought I should be in a mental home. She put her hands on me cheeks – I haven't shaved in days, like – and she said she was scared of me. I didn't know what to say, and then she said she liked me all the same. And she told me it was good to have got Tam out of the way. That was a lovely thing to say, I reckoned.

I pulled her close to me then, and kissed her belly. It was firm but soft too, and mostly smooth. But there were wee marks all over it, down her sides and up towards her chest. Wee healed-over scars, wee round ones and wee long ones. Everything from knife cuts to fag burns and fuck knows what. They were all like wee patterns and wounds from her past. I didn't think it was right to say anything about them. I've plenty too, and I don't really like to talk that much about how they got there. So I just started to tongue them a wee bit, and just kiss them because they were all parts of her lovely wee body. It was pretty horny, to be honest.

So I goes: 'Pull your skirt up.'

And she did. It was brilliant. She had on this wee white thong thing, just covering her pussy, just a wee tiny bit yellow at the front. Her legs were marked, up around the thighs, as if she'd been hurt there too. I put me hands on the wee wounds and dents on her body, running me fingers over them. Wee Blondie didn't mind. It was very personal, but she let me do what I wanted. I looked up and there were some tears in her eyes. I smiled and, to be honest, I knew there were tears in my eyes too. It was mad as fuck. Then she did a three-sixty twirl for me. Wee steel backside on her. Wee white cord running up between the cheeks. You could tell she'd been hurt on nearly every part of her body, so you could. Then she took off her wee top and showed her tits. No bra or nothing. There was a scar on one of her nipples.

I pulled her towards me and started kissing her again, all over her stomach and her wee boobs. I was sort of licking her and kissing her at the same time. I was rooted up by then and wanted to save touching her vagina until I got out of me clothes. I looked up and she was smiling, like she was happy enough. I was loving her, I promise you. I stood up and took off me gear anyway. She stood there, her hands sort of shaking by her sides, and just waited for me. I took off everything, and I was up like a fucken spire. It must've been three fucken weeks since I blew a load, and me nuts were dancing. I had this warm feeling all through me. There was no way I was going out of that room without emptying that fucken sack, even though in one way sack-emptying didn't seem that important. I sat down and she moved in forward to me again. I rubbed her thighs at the side. Then I started to slide me hand round her arse, and then down between at the back and then round the front. I tucked a finger under her thong and felt her vagina. It was hot, I'm telling you. I just looked up at her eyes then and she was smiling down at me, tears all over the place. She must've known I was dying about her.

Then she put her hand on me arm, right on the big scars where the flesh was grated off like worms years ago. She wasn't trying to stop me or nothing. She just wanted to run her fingers over the marks. To be honest, I don't know much about love, but I knew a wee bit of it was there just then. And she was liking it too. I knew that for a fact. If she hadn't been, I'd have gone.

I pulled her knickers up from the back then, up tight into her arse crack, and I could see them ride up into her hole in front of me. She had wee fawny hairs. All her hole was gathered into a wee bump in her thong and I couldn't help licking it, stains and all. Fuck knows where she'd been in her past, and fuck probably had a lot to do with it. But I couldn't give a shite. I just licked over the whole wee bump with the end of me tongue, and then with the whole thing. Then I pulled the thong down and exposed it all. It was like looking at a Van Gogh or some fucken shite that makes people go crazy with the beauty of it and all. It was mad just having me own wee personal moment with this cracking woman. And I just had to get me dick into her right then.

Normally I'd be one for more foreplay and all that shite, but I was busting for this. Really bad, like. She stepped out of her knickers and I pulled her wee hips down. She picked up this wee packet from the side table and ripped it open with her teeth. Dead cool, like. Then she just slipped the rubber on me with one hand. Dead professional, like. It felt good when she put it on. Then I just kissed her again and pulled her downwards a wee bit more. In no time her pussy was right on the end of me cock, and then slowly she was sliding down to end up sitting on me knee, facing me. I just held her there for a wee minute, leaning forward and kissing her tits. Then when I loosened me hands a bit, she started going up and down, but so slowly that it was like she didn't want to spill something. Each time she came down, I pulled at her, pulling her down hard onto me. And every time she went up, I just felt the long movement in her hips. I'm telling you, heaven couldn't be any better than that. In the back of me head I remember thinking maybe Karim was at the same thing somewhere with all his virgins. The whole thing just made me feel happy. Every bit of me was singing, so it was. Singing and dancing.

I'll be honest with you, so I will. I don't mind admitting that the earth didn't move for her. I don't think it even really trembled. But I think she was maybe just giving me something, to thank me in her own wee fucked-up way. That's the way she'd probably got things done when she was shacked up with The Cunt and Tam.

I was glad to take what she was offering anyway, and I hope she knows it meant a lot to me. It was the highlight of me life, so it was. I'd never be able to thank her enough for that there, but I'd give her whatever she wanted if I could get it.

So after about six or seven of her wee ups and downs, I couldn't hold it any longer. I had to pull her down, holding her close, hard and tight as I unloaded into her for fucken ages. It felt like that anyway. She kind of pushed up, as if she wanted to slide down me again, but I pulled her in so tight and so hard that I could feel her heartbeat on me head. I didn't shout like I sometimes do. I just sort of moaned like an oul dog, and me eyes all twisted up like I'd been hit over the head with a stick. It was a fucken mighty, cracking cum, I'm telling you. The juiciest I ever had. I mean, God help that girl. She must have thought I was going to faint or something.

So I gave her this big kiss and she stepped back. I just stared at her a wee bit, looking at her looking at me, and I could see she had some kind of wee tiny smile on her face. I grinned like a bastard, so I did. Biggest fucken grin you ever saw. Everything was just dead on then, so it was. We both just laughed a wee bit and she sort of stood there all awkward. I think if we'd known each other better we'd have hugged or something. She looked like she wanted a wee hug. I don't know.

I whipped the condom off and stood up. I stuck it in this oul cigarette packet on the table at the side of the bed and put it in me pocket. I didn't want to leave that oul crap with her. It would have been cheeky, like. I stood up and gave her this big smacker on the lips. Then I sort of hugged her, and she hugged me back. I knew she would. I told her she was a fucken star. I was feeling weak as fuck, but I was warm and happy. And I tell you now, being empty never felt so good as it did there and then. I just told her to remember she could tell the cops everything if she wanted and that I no longer gave a fuck. And I told her she should think about getting out of this city.

Then I just got me clothes back on and basically walked out. I knew she was a bit drunk and tired and she maybe felt she'd done her bit for me. I don't know. But I'd had some time with her and it was the best thing ever. I had too much to tell her if I was going to tell her anything, so I cut it short. I had to focus. She sort of put her hand out to me as I walked away, but I kept on walking.

I went down the stairs and opened the front door. I looked back up but she wasn't there. I hoped she didn't hate me right then, for just leaving like that. I took out the envelope with a grand of the reporter's money in it and just dropped it on the stairs and went.

It was cold as fuck outside. I didn't have a jacket anymore, so I just sort of huddled myself together and started walking. I kept on checking to see if anyone was following me, but I swear I couldn't see it if they were. The odd taxi with some drunk bastards shouting like fuck at me out the window were the only things that passed. Other than that, it was dead quiet.

I stopped at the bridge when I got into town, shivering like hell. I just sort of stared out over the river. I put the keys to me flat in the fag box that the oul rubber was in and fucked it into the water. I just walked on again after that. I was trying to make myself feel something for the oul town when I looked at that river, the oul Lagan that brought it here all them years back. But I couldn't think about that. I just felt too happy about me. That was as happy as I've ever been, so it was.

I arrived at the gates here about dawn. The security guard just waved me on in. I wouldn't have been able to get into the garage through the front entrance because it'd all be closed up, so I just went into the building with me security pass. I couldn't think of any reason why anyone would ask me questions, if anyone was even going to be around. We often do Saturday shifts, like. I walked on in, past another security guard and just kept on going. There were a couple of cleaning staff about, but I didn't look at any of them in case they thought something funny was going on. No one looked twice at me. They didn't even look once.

I'd to switch the lights on in the garage. It's dark as fuck here, even during the day. And usually cold as fuck too. The black Merc was still sitting here, clean as a whistle, fresh and ready to roll. I took a look around her and she's looking good as new, so she is. Beautiful as fuck. Then I went up to the Co-ordinator's office to look for the keys. His top drawer was locked, so I grabbed a big spanner from the garage and broke the fucker open. The keys were there all right, in an envelope marked D6–14, whatever that means. I put them in me pocket and sat back in Steven's chair and just kipped for a few hours before talking to you again. I'm rested now and ready to roll, big lad. Just give me a couple of minutes. I'm going to gather up some odds and ends and then we'll hit the road.

D6–14. March 20. Saturday.
11.51
Speaker(s): Woundlicker

Okay, Houston. We're ready for blast off. Ignition, and all
that crap. I'll talk again when I've something to say.

D6–14. March 20. Saturday.
16.17
Speaker(s): Woundlicker

Well, mucker? How's it hanging? How in the name of
fuck are you doing? Eh? Christ, this has been a blast
today, I promise you. Jesus fucken Christ on a bike, has
this been a blast? It's been hard fucken labour, so it has,
but good honest work too. I'm tougher than you'd think,
you know. When I put me mind to it, I can stretch
myself and get some shite accomplished, so I can. Fletcher
the Stretcher, eh?

So here anyway. Let me put it like this. There was a
wedding reception today at a hotel up the Holywood
Road, right? It's still going on and all. Looks like it could
shape up to be a half decent party, to be honest. So oul
Fletcher invited himself along for the crack. I gatecrashed
the thing, you know. No one could tell or anything. Sure
who the fuck knows who half the people are at a
wedding? There's about a hundred at it, I'd say. A
hundred loyalists and unionists and Protestants or
whatever you want to call the guests. But there's one less
at it now. I don't know how long it'll be before the rest
of them catch on, but one man is definitely missing. You
can be sure of that.

So I'd walked on into this thing earlier, looking as
dapper as I ever did in me dirty suit and trainers. A couple
of funny looks and all, but that was the height of it. I got a
wee drink at the bar, just a wee orange, and stood there so
I could get me bearings. Calm before the storm sort of

thing. I didn't know who the fuck the bride and groom were. Dodgy enough looking, so they were. He was already blocked. Probably the only way he could cope with what he'd just done. His new wife was dead pregnant, smoking away at the B&H and drinking oul shitty champagne and talking bollocks. And, in case you want to know, the bride wore orange, so she did. On her face.

Then I clocked me oul DUP pal Lionel Rosborough. Dear oul Lionel. Dear oul Lionel, who had me put out of house and home, and had me arm grated like a block of cheese. Me oul pal, eh? He was standing there slabbering to some bloke with Rangers earrings about the ways of the world or some bollocks like that. I kept me distance anyway and made sure no one knew I was looking at him. It's like the spying business you're in, you know. You don't have to look at someone to keep your eye on them, so you don't.

There was a bunch of well-known faces there, to be honest. A few other DUP ones and some as well from one of the loyalist parties, the one linked to the UVF or some shite. One of them Ulster Scots language dickheads was there too. You know the one who goes on that he can speak it fluent and all, when it's just a fucken accent? Aye, that bollocks. And I knew a bunch of others to see from the telly or whatever, or from going round shouting during the elections. I was hardly star-struck or anything. Cunt-struck, maybe.

So there they were, all hob-nobbing and talking about another wee orange baby on the way and all that. It'll be a smoker, I don't doubt. Then some long-faced woman with a blue hat on her asked me at the bar if I was a friend of Robin's. I says aye, we used to be in prison together and all. She didn't know what to say. Then she says she was his

Auntie Jane. I said Robin had told me all about her and that he used to fancy her when he was a wee lad. Silly cow didn't know where to look then. Fuck her if she can't take a joke anyway.

To be honest, I was feeling as right as rain. I think that shag had cleared the system out a bit. Cleaned all the pipes, you know. I was dead focused. My advice to boxers would be to get their hole the night before a fight, so it would. It puts sex in the background. That's priceless when you've a bunch of shite to deal with, so it is.

After about half an hour anyway, Lionel goes to the jacks. It was only a matter of time, sort of thing. He was boozing away. Drinks a lot for a holy man, so he does. I walked on in after him. Some other wanker was taking a piss too and Lionel was saying to him that the bride was looking really well. To him, she probably fucken was. So I went up and stood there, pretending to take a slash. Then the other bloke said he'd see Lionel later and walked out.

I goes: 'Mr Rosborough?'

He's like: 'Aye?'

I says: 'I'm Ian. I work up in Stormont. Can we have a wee chat? Something I think you'd be interested in.'

So he just sort of nodded and zipped up and went and washed his hands. I zipped up and went over to the sinks too.

I says: 'Is that all right with you?'

He's like: 'Is it important? I'm at a function here.'

I goes: 'So am I. I'm a mate of Robin's.'

He's like: 'Oh right. He's a good lad.'

I says: 'Aye. The best.' Then I goes: 'It's pretty important. I heard you'd be here and I wanted to show you something. Documents, you know.'

He goes: 'What sort of documents?'

I says: 'Found them in a car, the one the Prime Minister used when he was over last week.'

He says: 'Well shouldn't you be returning them to him?'

I says: 'I was going to, but I took a wee peek at them and they're all about your man Tam and the other Provie fella, The Cunt. The ones who were killed.'

He goes: 'Was the Prime Minister not here before those murders?'

I says: 'Aye he was. That's the fucken thing. They're named in the documents, so they are. It's like they knew about the murders before they happened, so it is.'

He goes: 'What do you mean, named?'

I says: 'There's just all their details and pictures and all. It says something about them both being well known in their communities and that there's some rogue element that's planning to kill paramilitaries and all.'

He says: 'Rogue element?'

I goes: 'Aye. It's all intelligence stuff. To be honest, I haven't read it all. I don't read too well.'

He's like: 'I see. Are you being serious, Ian?'

'Aye. Dead serious. Honest to fuck.'

'Why are you telling me?'

'I just know you from up our way. I'd trust you and all.'

He goes: 'Does anyone know you have them?'

'No. Just me. I didn't say a word to anyone. I was going to give them to some journalist but then I thought it might be better to give them to you.'

He's like: 'Right. And what do you think they say?'

I says: 'I don't know. I just thought it was weird that those two were killed and that the Prime Minister had been reading about them just before it. He knew about some rogue element and all. Tam was killed the day after he left.'

Your man says: 'That's very true. Dirty war stuff? Is that what you're thinking?'

I says: 'Aye. Must be. Some kind of set-up maybe, to get the politicians facing the same enemy or something. Fuck knows.'

So then he goes: 'Do I know you from somewhere?' He hasn't seen me in ten years, like.

I'm like: 'I've gone to hear you speak a few times. Maybe that's it.' He liked that.

Then he goes: 'Where are these documents, Ian?' I had to laugh at him calling me Ian.

So I says: 'I have them outside. Locked in the car.'

He was dead excited and all, so he was. I could see he was trying to play it cool, but he was busting to get them.

I just says: 'It'll take me two seconds if you want to see them.'

And he goes: 'Just in the car park, is it?'

'Aye.'

'I'll go with you.'

The fucker just walked into it, so he did. Easy fucken peasy. I headed out to the side of the car park and he followed me like a wee puppy. He was saying it was a nice day to get married and all this bollocks.

We got up to the side of the car anyway and he's all amazed, so he is.

He goes: 'Nice set of wheels there, Ian. Government issue?'

I'm like: 'Aye. We're allowed to borrow them some-times. This is the one the Prime Minister was in, so it is.'

He goes: 'Aye. I think I've seen it before.'

I looked all around me, and he did the same. Then he says: 'It's all right. There's no one around.'

So I says: 'Thanks.' Then I hit him with me wee claw

hammer. I just drew it from me pocket and spun round and clocked the fucker on the side of the head, hard as fuck. It was brilliant to see the look on his face. He didn't go down straight away. He kind of rocked on his feet a wee bit, stunned to fuck. It still must've looked like the two of us were just standing there in our suits, drunk as fuck and talking shite about the wedding. I looked round anyway and there was still no one about.

He goes: 'What the fuck?' His eyes were wandering all over the show. He starts rubbing his head.

I goes: 'Fuck up, you prick.' Then I gave him this sweet upper cut. Caught him square under the gob, bouncing his head back, knocking this wee patch of a wig straight off him. He hit the ground then. Just a big heap of Lionel, so he was. A big heap of fucken shite. He was half out of it. He was moaning and all. I loved it, so I did.

Me oul mucker Artie Kill-A-Man Callaghan got the same thing about an hour later, so he did. Oul Artie, eh? Made sure I got the fuck kicked out of me that time, so he did. Got that house bricked in Twinbrook and all. Got me petrol bombed, so he did. Sent me on the run, so he did. Oul Artie, eh?

I'd found out where he'd be that day too. He was giving a speech up in Ardoyne about the stuff in the news and all. The Shinners had their boys put up one of their platforms and got an oul Tricolour draped over it and all. Then they went round the houses making sure hundreds of people turned up and everything. I seen them rounding them up, so I did. I just walked into the back of the crowd to listen. Some slapper spoke first, welcoming everyone in Irish and all that.

Then she goes: 'It's too much for the British to see us lead this peace process,' and all this here. She goes: 'That's why they're having their agents in the loyalist community attack and kill our leading lights.'

You could see the anger in the place. They're going to go tearing the fucken joint up after that. The traffic lights are for it tonight, so they are. Then she introduced Artie Callaghan, calling him a champion of human rights and Irish freedom. She wasn't even taking the piss. Artie put this wee pair of round glasses on him before he came up on stage.

He goes: 'When we cry out for peace, the British blind our children. Just ask the family of Seanie Latimer.' Then he's all: 'When we honour those who work for peace, the British kill them. Just ask the family of Eamon The Count Cleary.'

And then he goes: 'And the loyalists have the audacity to blame the volunteers of the IRA for taking the life of one of their twisted UDA pimps?'

He's all like: 'They claim a republican volunteer was doing backstreet deals with a loyalist drug dealer and poisoning our own youth.' He made The Cunt out to be a real hero. I always thought heroes did noble things, know what I mean?

Anyway, everyone was going for it, cheering and all. Oul Artie is smart, like. He makes the IRA sound like they just love peace and nothing else. What the fuck, like. And I love the way he said Cunt was a hero. I really adore that, so I do. Wee Blondie would have got a kick out of that one.

Anyway, he slabbered on for about ten minutes before saying something else in Irish and going off the stage. I tuned out after a while, so I did, and just started looking round me and all.

So then at the end, I walked up and caught him as

some journalist was asking if the peace process was at risk. Artie was saying the lust for a settlement was too strong and all, but that he wouldn't be surprised if the people took to the streets and everything. Let's have a big fucken riot, in other words.

I collared him after that and told him I worked up in Stormont. Same oul bollocks about finding the documents in the car and the government knowing about some rogue element and all. He couldn't resist it, like.

He goes: 'That's interesting, Hugh.'

And then he goes: 'Do I know you from somewhere?'

I didn't want to say I'd stared at him bollock naked from the flat that night, or that he'd made sure I got the fuck kicked out of me for saying I'd vote Monster Raving Loony.

So I goes: 'I've been to hear you speak a load of times, so I have. Maybe that's it.' He fell for that bit, too, the wanker.

It was awkward because there were loads of those heroes around the place. All the tattooed fuckwits of the day were up there. I told him the car was over the street and he called on some big bastard to come with him. I didn't know what to say, so the three of us just walked on over.

When we got to the car he goes: 'Nice motor.'

I says I borrowed it for the day, and it was the one the Prime Minister goes round in and all. Then I had this wee idea, to get rid of the fucken ape. I said I didn't want to mention it earlier, but that one of the men in the crowd is a spook. I said it's this ex-SAS fucker who briefs the Prime Minister and all when he's over. Artie was busting to hear more about that.

He says: 'Are you sure?'

I says: 'Aye. His name's Steven. He was in the Army for years, undercover and all, and they reckon he knows the Provies inside out.'

Artie asked me where he was and what he was wearing and all this stuff. I just described the clothes of this drunk fucker I'd been standing beside in the crowd. I said he was armed and all. Artie turns to the cunt with him.

He says: 'Go and have a look, Neville. See what he's up to. I might want a wee word. Make sure you get pictures of him here as well. Our friend Hugh here might just be very helpful to us today.' I felt like laughing into his face, so I did.

Anyway, Neville nodded and just walked off straight away. I went round the other side of the car and Artie just followed after me. Another wee puppy, so he was. He took his specs off just when he thought I was going to get the keys and take the documents out.

That's when I hit him with the hammer. I cracked him right on the forehead and he fell back into this knackered oul bush at the side of the street. The specs went flying.

He goes: 'Jesus fuck.'

Then he starts kicking out at me. I pushed his legs away and cracked him on the head again. It was like killing a fish or something. He kicked a bit more then, but he was losing it. I punched the fucker in the face a few times and he sort of started to go limp. He was half out of it, so he was. And that's basically what's happened to Artie and Lionel so far today.

Now, mate, I've just got to finish the job. That's the two of them I have there, in the back seat. They're tied up fucken tight and all. Bound and gagged with oul rags from the garage, so they are. They're waiting to see what kind of cunt wee Fletcher Fee will turn out to be. Isn't that right, lads? Well I hope youse are feeling optimistic about all this, because I'm not. I fear the worst for the two of you, so I do. The very worst. Hands up who says you're not fucked. Oh, oops. Didn't mean to restrict your right to have your say, boys. My fault. I forgot that your fucken hands are tied to your feet. Silly me. And I forgot that your feet are tied to a bar underneath the front seats. Silly oul me, eh? Fletcher the Forgetter, eh?

You know, the thing that I love about this car is how fucken secure it is. I mean, in a whole load of different ways. We're parked now right in front of the City Hall watching the world go by. The Peelers probably wouldn't bother us, even if there were any about. Aye, the windows are blacked out and all, but if they ran the number in they'd soon find out it's a government motor. No one's going to come near it. But it's solid as fuck too. It's bulletproof and bombproof, so it can take any shite hitting it from outside. Nothing can get in. It's too strong. Something tells me that nothing's going to be able to get out either.

There's a full can of petrol on the passenger seat. There's one at Artie's feet and one at Lionel's feet in the back as well. Open cans, so they are. The smell in here would get you high, so it would. It's great. I'm just going to spill a wee bit of petrol on the passenger carpet here, and a wee taste on the seat too. I reckon when I light it, it'll take a couple of minutes to find the can in the front, and then when that goes up, it'll not be long finding the ones in the back too. Chain reaction, sort of thing. No one outside will even see a fucken spark. And it'll be a while before the smoke starts to get out through the doors. As I say, this bastard is sealed as tight as a crow's arse. You could just get all burned up in here and no one would notice at all.

Let's be honest about this from the start, lads. You're

fucked. I won't be here to see it, but I've a fair idea of the kind of shite you're about to go through. It's not going to be pretty, so it's not, although I suppose that depends on your point of view. That's the way it is in Northern Ireland, eh? One man's hero is another man's bastard. That's just part of life, eh?

So, my friend, I'm going to go now and just leave you to it. You know the deal. You know the crack here. You know where we all are. You know what's going to happen. Do what you want. Personally, I'd let the fuckers burn. There's fuck all to lose, when you think about it. Well, you'll lose this car, and that's a real shame. But sometimes you just have to sacrifice something.

As for me, I'm away to fuck. What can I tell you? Well, you can trust me when I say that I'll deny we ever met if anyone ever asks, which they won't. Why would they? My advice to you is to deny you ever heard one fucken word I said. No one can say otherwise, as long as you've played your cards right. And so far, I think that's just what you've done. I'm not exactly being hunted down or anything, and maybe that's the best thing for all of us. I don't want to have to start telling people that you're still listening in on politicians.

All that's left for me now is to turn round, cut the rags that are gagging these bastards, light the petrol and, basically, fuck off. Good luck to you, mate. I mean that. It's been fucken great knowing you, even if you are a cunt. And good luck too, Lionel and Artie. Youse might remember me from the past and youse might not, but that doesn't matter. At least youse know who I am now, eh? Too right. Cheerio.

D6–14. March 20. Saturday.
16.30
Speaker(s): Callaghan, Rosborough.

Callaghan: 'Jesus Christ.'
Rosborough: 'Help! Here in the car.'
Callaghan: 'Help.'
Rosborough: 'Hel…'

STATION D6:
COMMENTARY AND ANALYSIS

D6–14 imploded at 16.42. Firefighters were on the scene eleven minutes later and the fire within the vehicle was extinguished at 17.03. Pathologists believe Callaghan and Rosborough died from a combination of smoke inhalation and intense heat some three minutes after their final words.

After cutting the gags and alighting from the vehicle, Fletcher Fee [Woundlicker] was observed making his way casually through the grounds of City Hall, exiting at Donegall Square West. He walked along Bedford Street and onto the Dublin Road towards Shaftesbury Square. His movements were not tracked beyond there.

In the aftermath, a number of media investigations claimed the events of that day occurred in highly unusual circumstances. The Police Ombudsman was asked to investigate why a city centre patrol was called to other duties seven minutes after D6–14 arrived at the gates of City Hall. Questions were also raised as to why Fee had not been successfully approached by police following the death of his colleague, Karim Mohammed Khalid.

Each of these points was thoroughly investigated and any suggestion of government or security force complicity in the events of that day has been entirely dismissed by all official sources. The idea of complicity, in light of the recent political complications, has been viewed as fanciful in the extreme.

Fee had at no time been aggressively sought for questioning. He had chosen not to speak with police in the days after the death of Karim Khalid, and this clear wish had been respected. At no time had Fee been a suspect in the murders of Mr Samuel 'Tam' Long or Eamon 'The Count/The Cunt' Cleary. However, police are no longer looking for anyone else in connection with these killings. At all times, the government has made it clear, Fee acted alone.

A packaged pistol, likely to have belonged to Samuel 'Tam' Long, has since been intercepted en route to Algiers by HM Customs officials working to Security Service advice.

A further question raised following an investigation by the media was why no action was taken after a Stormont security guard reported D6–14 leaving the estate prior to the killing of Rosborough and Callaghan. An internal probe concluded this was down to poor communication between elements within the Northern Ireland Office. The NIO subsequently vowed it would urgently address this issue.

Since that day the government has increased the drive for cohesion in light of the vicious attacks on both sides of the community by Fee, who is helpfully being portrayed by the media as a drink- and drug-crazed killer. One description, sourced from the NIO media department and fed to the press, is that he is an unbalanced misfit who is 'harmed and dangerous'. The press have seized on this phrase.

The government has insisted Fee's killing spree must not be allowed to derail the desire for a lasting peace, for paramilitary disarmament and accountable regional government. It has said that these things are within the grasp of the people, and that Fee's deeds should serve to refocus minds on these goals. It has made it clear that it very much regrets the deaths of Mr Rosborough and Mr Callaghan, as well as those of Mr Cleary and Mr Long.

The government has been delighted to welcome representatives of all Northern Ireland political parties to Downing Street for urgent and significant talks regarding the security situation and the forwarding of the peace process. It notes with enthusiasm that in light of recent events – and of March 20 in particular – each party has unequivocally recommitted itself to finding a lasting final settlement to the continuing sectarian disputes which have bedevilled Northern Ireland society prior to and since the paramilitary cea﹍fires.

The government is very keen to maintain what it hopes is a vigorous new spirit in the search for peace. By continuing to work towards this goal, the government believes it can ultimately dilute the sectarian passions which endure throughout the state. The government has spoken of a new clarity of purpose, and all sides appear to have re-engaged with that in mind.

Privately, the government retains the opinion that the entire Woundlicker episode has, when placed alongside the political stalemate and its sectarian outworkings of recent times, been useful.

There have been no positive sightings of Fletcher Fee in Northern Ireland, the Republic of Ireland or elsewhere since March 20. It is known that he did not have a passport, but it is believed that this is no guarantee that he is still on the island of Ireland. He has not accessed his bank account. It had been depleted of funds prior to March 20. Fee made his escape with a total of some £1,050.

On March 27, Miss Molly Duddy disappeared. Police had made four calls to her Ardoyne home as the investigation into her lover's murder continued, although they had remained satisfied she had no involvement in that killing. A neighbour informed officers on March 28 that Miss Duddy had left her home the previous day with a small suitcase. On a subsequent search of the property they discovered a handwritten letter, postmarked from Belfast, dated March 23. It read:

'Well Molly. You'll have heard about all the shite that went on up the town by now. Those cunts Rosborough and Callaghan. You probably didn't know them but I knew the fuckers all right. Same as you knew Cunt and Tam. I'm glad they're dead. I hope you got the grand I left you that night round your house. The money's dead safe to use. I have to be invisible as fuck and I'm safe where I am now. But not for long so I'll be moving on. I've it all planned out and there's no worries.

I want to ask you to come with me. I know it sounds mad as fuck and all, but it's the thing I most want. I sort of fell for you a while back and I'd love to spend more time with you. I'm not as mad as you maybe think I am. To be honest, I just went through a bit of a bad patch and threw the head up. But I'm fine now. I'm not really a murderer. If you want to see me, even to chat about it, then meet me at the back of Queen's University, the main building bit, at about noon on Saturday. I'll look all different and all, but you'll know me.

Don't worry as no one knows that we've ever even spoke, except me and you. You'll not get arrested or nothing. If you don't show, then no problem. But I'd love to see you there. Maybe we can make a bit of a life together somewhere else. Give it a chance and I'll love you forever. If not, then dead on. I'll love you forever anyway. See you later Wee Blondie. Fletcher x.'

Report compiled exclusively by
Glover Steven Brand
D6 Station Co-ordinator

ENDS